Meow

A SCREENPLAY

by

Taylor St. Sauvage Brandon

&

Niko Zinovii

Zinovii Art Studio

Santa Monica, California

chalkos

Meow

All events, humans, cats and other animals in this tale are fictitious, the product of this author's imagination. Any resemblance to actual humans, cats, dogs or other animals, living or dead, is entirely coincidental. All places referenced are either fictitious or actual but used fictitiously.

Published by: Zinovii Art Studio
Santa Monica, California
www.zinoviiartstudio.com

ISBN: 978-0-9900085-5-2 (trade paperback)

LCCN: 2023910788

Interior art by: Leonardo Ariel Ariza Ardila
Cover art by: Leonardo Ariel Ariza Ardila

First Edition, 2023
Printed in the United States of America

Dedication

The publication of this screenplay is dedicated to its co-author Taylor and his family, may they have as much adventurous family fun in real life as the characters of this script had in their one magical night.

Contents

A Note on the Screenplay

The screenplay that follows is reproduced in its entirety and unaltered, with only slight adjustments made to its original format in order to provide greater ease of reading; specifically, script page numbers and scene numbers have been eliminated, as have all the uses of "(CONTINUED)" and "CONTINUED:" and "MORE" that delineate the continuation of scenes and dialogue across ordinal pages.

As this book is of a smaller size than a standard 8 ½" x 11" screenplay, each page of script no longer represents one minute of screen time. (The *Meow* screenplay in its original 8 ½" x 11" size is 104 pages in length.)

EXT indicates an outdoor scene, INT and indoor scene. O.S. is an abbreviation for "off screen." V.O. is an abbreviation for "voice over."

Act One

FADE IN:

INT. FELICIA'S YARD - NIGHT

The moon is full and its yellow glow is illuminating the old wooden fence that is directly in front of it.

CREDITS BEGIN

A dirty, scraggly **ALLEY CAT** hops up upon the fence. It appears solid black against the moon in the background. After a moment, a second **CAT** walks into the picture, moving along the top of the fence. It stops mere inches in front of the first cat.

There is a moment of silence as the cats eye each other. Then, simultaneously, they let out their infantile cat **CRIES**, each trying to claim the fence as their own.

The **TITLE "MEOW"** appears on the screen. After it is read by the audience, it disappears.

Continuing their feline crying, the cats are both refusing to give ground.

The two cats are upon a high fence that

is separating two homes in a middle class suburban neighborhood. An eight year old boy, **CHRISTOPHER**, is peering out a lit window from one of the adjacent houses. His attention is focused on the arguing cats. A young girl's voice is heard off screen.

JAN (O.S.)
Come-on Christopher, it's your turn.

INT. CHRISTOPHER'S BEDROOM - NIGHT

Christopher turns away from the window to face **JAN**, his eleven year old sister. She is sitting upon the floor in front of a Yatzee game which they are playing.

CHRISTOPHER
But the cats are fighting again.

JAN
So?

CHRISTOPHER
So I wanna watch them.

JAN
But we're in the middle of a game.

Christopher turns back to the window.

CHRISTOPHER
I don't care, I wanna
watch them.

JAN
Oh, you're so immature.

Their mother, **FELICIA**, steps into the room. She is carefully putting on an earring and wearing a very nice dress. She is blonde, attractive and approximately 35 years old.

FELICIA
Of course he's immature
Jan, he's only eight
years old.

JAN
So, that doesn't mean
that he gets to get his
way. He's always quitting
in the middle of a game.

Smiling, Felicia is moving across the room.

FELICIA
Come-on Christopher.

CHRISTOPHER
But Mom, I want to watch
the cats fight.

Reaching her son, Felicia starts to guide him away from the window and back towards the game.

FELICIA
Now Christopher, you're
in the middle of a game
with your sister. After
you finish, well, then
you can watch the cats
fight.

Reluctantly sitting down next to his sister, Christopher thinks for a second and then looks up at his mother.

CHRISTOPHER
Mom, how come those cats
make those noises? Sounds
weird, like babies
crying.

Thinking for a moment, Felicia's smile broadens.

FELICIA
Well, that's how they
talk to each other.

CHRISTOPHER
Talk to each other? Sounds like they're screaming at each other.

FELICIA
Well, they are fighting, aren't they?

Turning, she heads back towards the door.

FELICIA (CONT'D)
Better finish your game before Aunt Jeannie comes up to tuck you in. It's getting late.

She glances at her wristwatch.

FELICIA (CONT'D)
And I'd better get moving or I'm going to be late.

Jan smiles.

JAN
Is he handsome Mom?

Felicia's smile drops.

FELICIA
I'll find out soon.

Leaving the bedroom, their mother closes the door. After a moment of silence:

CHRISTOPHER

Do you think he'll be our new dad?

Thinking about it, Jan lets out a somewhat frustrated sigh.

JAN

... I don't know.

CREDITS END

INT. LIVING ROOM - NIGHT

JEANNIE, Felicia's dark haired sister is watching TV. She is a year or two older than Felicia. Moving down the stairs, Felicia steps down into the living room. She does not look enthusiastic about her date. Smiling, Jeannie moves to her.

JEANNIE

All ready?

FELICIA

I guess so.

JEANNIE

Oh, come on Felicia, you

should be looking forward to this. Hey, for all you know this could turn out to be the most exciting night of your life.

FELICIA
But I don't know anything about him. I don't even know what he looks like.

JEANNIE
Hey, don't be so pessimistic about blind dates. That's how I met Bill you know. Yeah, yeah, I know, it was an ugly divorce but it was a great marriage.

Felicia just gives her a look.

JEANNIE (CONT'D)
Felicia, look honey, you gotta get back into the swing of things. You date what, maybe once every four months? God, how do you expect to reel anybody in when you're not even putting your hook in the water?

Jeannie glances down at Felicia's dress.

JEANNIE (CONT'D)
Maybe you should put on a shorter dress. You've got nice legs. You gotta bait the hook too you know.

FELICIA
Hook, bait, reel him in. You make romance sound like... like deep-sea fishing.
(exhales/a beat)
Look Jeannie, you're my sister and I know that you're only trying to help but... romance ... it ... it's just not part of my life anymore. I've given up on it. There's no Prince Charming waiting out there for me.

Jeannie looks at her sister seriously.

JEANNIE
Felicia... Mike died six years ago. God bless his soul, I loved him too, but you didn't have to bury that part of

yourself with him.
(a beat)
You need to find someone to love again. Someone to love you. A husband. A father for your kids.

There is a brief moment of silence between them which is interrupted by the doorbell RINGING.

At once, Jeannie begins to move her sister towards the door,smiling and talking rapidly.

JEANNIE (CONT'D)
Okay, okay, here he is. He's a real nice guy, works in the accounting department at the office. Real bright. Sure, he's not a looker, but...

Pulling open the door, Jeannie widens her smile and raises her voice, greeting Felicia's date, **EUGENE**. On the short side, he is in his late 30s and nerdy looking. Dressed in a polyester suit and wearing glasses, his hair is neatly parted to one side. Appearing nervous, he is holding something behind his back. Seeing Eugene, Felicia's face drops.

JEANNIE (CONT'D)
Eugene! It's nice to see you. Come in, come in. Eugene, this is Felicia. Felicia, Eugene.

Stepping into the apartment, he pulls a slightly flattened bouquet of flowers out from behind his back, offering them to Felicia.

EUGENE
(nervous)
Hi. Th-these are for you. Sorry they're a little crumpled. I, ah, I accidentally sat on them.

Felicia gives her sister a disappointed look. Smiling, Jeannie simply shrugs her shoulders.

INT. CHRISTOPHER'S BEDROOM - NIGHT

Christopher and Jan are standing in front of and looking out of the room's windows.

CHRISTOPHER
Can you see him?

JAN
Shhh!!! No, not yet.

They hear their home's front door open and close and then they see their mother walking with her date towards a car parked in the street. They are disappointed.

CHRISTOPHER
Wow, he's shorter than Mom.

JAN
He... he looks kind of goofy.

JEANNIE (O.S.)
Spying on your Mom, huh?

Surprised, the kids turn around to see their Aunt standing in the room's doorway. Letting loose a smile, she rushes up to the window.

JEANNIE (CONT'D)
Move over.

EXT. FELICIA'S HOUSE - NIGHT

Jeannie and the two children are looking out one of Christopher's bedroom windows. On the sidewalk, Eugene accidentally steps into a pile of dog excrement. Immediately, he begins to quickly and nervously rub his shoe clean by scrapping it against the curb. Felicia tries to pretend not to notice.

INT. CHRISTOPHER'S BEDROOM - NIGHT

Jeannie and the children are still looking out of the window.

JEANNIE

Looks like it's going to be a long night for your mom kids.

JAN

He's not going to be our new dad, is he?

JEANNIE

No, I don't think so. Just a date. Sort of a warm up for your mom 'till she finds her Prince Charming.

JAN

Is that ever going to happen?

JEANNIE
Of course it'll happen...
(skeptical)
One day.

Jeannie decides to quickly change the subject, pointing the moon out to the kids.

JEANNIE (CONT'D)
Oh, hey, look, the moon's full. You know what that means.

CHRISTOPHER
What?

Moving the kids away from the window, Jeannie guides Christopher towards his bed.

JEANNIE
"What?" Didn't your Mom tell you about a full moon? When there's a full moon in the sky...
Beware.

She starts tucking Christopher into bed.

JEANNIE (CONT'D)
The moon does a lot more

than make the tide go in and out you know. It does all sorts of "things".

Jan glances back towards the window.

JAN
(doesn't like the idea)
Like make people fall in love?

Jeannie turns her eyes to Jan. There is brief moment of silence.

JEANNIE
Don't worry, the moon's not going to make your mom fall in love with her "goofy" date.

She quickly turns back to Christopher, hamming it up.

JEANNIE (CONT'D)
But, it is going to make some people act a little strange. And most importantly, it's going to make "things" happen that don't normally happen.

CHRISTOPHER
Like what?

JAN
Like werewolves?

Jeannie nods her head.

JEANNIE
Yep, werewolves. And lots of other "things".

Taking Jan by the hand, Jeannie begins to lead her out of the bedroom.

JEANNIE (CONT'D)
"Things" we don't even know about.

Reaching the door, she looks back at Christopher and smiles, dropping her campy act.

JEANNIE (CONT'D)
Sleep tight, don't let the werewolves bite.

Flicking off the light, Jeannie begins to HUM the theme song from "The Twilight Zone" aloud. Leaving with Jan, she closes the door. Alone in the dark, Christopher sinks down into his blankets and looks out at the night's full moon.

CHRISTOPHER
... Werewolves ...

He HEARS a cat screech out from somewhere outside.

EXT. FELICIA'S YARD - NIGHT

Leaping over the fence, one **CAT** is fleeing from **ANOTHER CAT**.

They both disappear into the neighbor's yard. The chasing cat is the one screeching out.

EXT. FRANK'S BACK YARD - NIGHT

The fleeing cat stops and turns to face its pursuer. Standing with their faces an inch apart, they start crying at each other like wild babies. The garage, way in the back of the deep yard, is open and a light is on within it.

INT. GARAGE - NIGHT

The garage is very large and most of it is dark.

A lean, hard looking man is lying beneath a jacked up car, working on it. He is wearing a mechanic's one piece outfit which has the name "FRANK" on the front of it. Hearing the screeching cats, he stops what he is doing and looks out into the yard behind him.

FRANK
Damn cats.
(a beat / yelling)
WINSTON!... WINSTON!

WINSTON, a large brown and white bulldog is sleeping on the floor besides the car. He is snoring.

FRANK (CONT'D)
(yelling)
WINSTON!

Winston awakes, quickly rolling to its large paws. Hearing the crying cats, the dog immediately takes off out of the garage with murder in its brutal eyes. Under the car, Frank goes back to work.

FRANK (CONT'D)
(chuckling)
Good boy Winston! Go get'em.

Frank stops what he is doing as he sees something out of the corner of his eye - several **RATS** scurrying through the darkness on the other side of the garage.

FRANK (CONT'D)
Damn rats...

EXT. FRANK'S BACK YARD - NIGHT

Running up the driveway, Winston starts barking as he gets within sight of the cats. They immediately take off. The bulldog locks his eyes onto the closest one and starts chasing it.

Both animals disappear into the darkness.

EXT. FELICIA'S YARD - NIGHT

Leaping on top of the fence separating the two yards, the cat that Winston did not give chase to balances itself and slowly turns its shiny eyes up to the night's glowing moon.

A moment passes.

INT. LIVING ROOM - NIGHT

Jeannie is resting in a reclining chair, watching TV and eating popcorn. Hearing the jingling of keys and a lock turning, she turns to the front door. It opens and in walks Felicia. From the expression on her face, it is obvious that she did not have an enjoyable date. Jeannie sits up.

JEANNIE
You're back early.
(knowing the answer)
... How did things go?

FELICIA
Don't even ask.

JEANNIE
That bad, huh?

FELICIA
Worse.

JEANNIE
Well, just don't give up.

FELICIA
I already have.
(a beat)
I'll be down in a minute.

Turning, she heads to the stairs, ascending them. Letting out a sigh, Jeannie sinks back into her seat.

INT. HALLWAY - NIGHT

Coming up the stairs, Felicia moves down the dimly lit hall, quietly opening a closed door.

INT. CHRISTOPHER'S BEDROOM - NIGHT

Peeking in at her son, she sees that he is asleep. Managing a smile, she silently pulls the door closed.

INT. JAN'S BEDROOM - NIGHT

Jan is lying in bed asleep. Next to her is a large bird cage containing a yellow **CANARY**. After a moment, the door to the room silently opens and her mother looks in at her.

Seeing that her daughter is asleep, she starts to pull the door closed but stops as she hears:

JAN (O.S.)
Mom, is that you?

Stepping into the room, Felicia moves towards her daughter.

FELICIA
I thought you were asleep.

JAN
Did you like him Mom?

Felicia thinks for a second.

FELICIA
He was nice but I won't be seeing him again.

Jan smiles.

JAN
Good. He looked goofy.

Felicia laughs.

FELICIA
He was.

Jan starts laughing. The Canary awakens and flutters its wings.

FELICIA (CONT'D)
Oh, I see Polly's awake too. She's looking a lot better.

JAN
Yeah, she's all better thanks to you Mom.

FELICIA

Well, you're lucky your mom's a vet.

A cat SCREECHES out somewhere outside. Polly immediately takes off, flapping about her cage.

JAN

Boy, those stray cats really scare Polly Mom.

FELICIA

Well, don't worry. As long as she's in the house she's safe.

(a beat)

Well honey, it's late. You'd better get to sleep.

Pulling the blankets up to her daughter's chin, Felicia kisses Jan upon the forehead and then exits the room.

INT. LIVING ROOM - NIGHT

Jeannie rises from her chair to answer the RINGING phone as Felicia moves down the stairs into the living room.

JEANNIE

Hello?

Jeannie is listening to whoever is on the other line.

FELICIA

Who is it?

JEANNIE

(into the phone)

Hold on.

She covers the phone's receiver with a hand.

JEANNIE (CONT'D)

(to Felicia)

It's your answering service. You want me to tell them you're not in?

Concerned, Felicia moves over to the phone.

FELICIA

No, I'll take it.

She takes the phone.

FELICIA (CONT'D)

Hello?

(listening)
Mrs. Mullan? Her cat?
(a beat / listening)
Call her and tell her to meet me at my office in fifteen minutes.
(a beat / listening)
Yes.
(a beat / listening)
Okay, I'm leaving now.

Hanging up the phone, she starts to look around the room for her car keys.

FELICIA (CONT'D)
Jeannie, can you stay a little longer? I've got an emergency, a cat got hit by a car.

Finding her car keys, she picks them up.

JEANNIE
Sure, sure, no problem. It's getting late, I'll probably end up sleeping over anyway.

FELICIA
Thanks, I really appreciate this.

Felicia heads towards the front door.

JEANNIE

Hey, don't worry about it. You just do what you have to do.

FELICIA

Thanks.

She leaves.

EXT. FELICIA'S HOUSE - NIGHT

Walking down her front sidewalk, Felicia is moving towards her car which is parked in the street. As she steps onto the sidewalk, she shuffles to a stop as a screeching **BLACK CAT** zooms by her, taking off across her lawn. Hearing hard nails scratching upon the sidewalk, she turns to see the cat's pursuer, Winston, turn its eyes from the fleeing cat to her. Barking loudly, the dog forgets about the cat and now charges her.

Eyes bulging, Felicia races to her car with Winston right on her heels. Somehow, she manages to jump into the car and SLAM its door shut just before Winston can take a bite out of her.

INT. FELICIA'S CAR - NIGHT

Barking loudly, Winston backs away from the car so that he can look in at Felicia. Exhaling deeply, she nervously sticks a key into the car's ignition and starts the engine.

EXT. FELICIA'S HOUSE - NIGHT

His eyes still focused on Felicia, Winston is continuing his mad barking.

INT. FELICIA'S CAR - NIGHT

Turning her eyes back towards the bulldog, Felicia sees the animal's owner, Frank, slowly walking up behind the dog. He is grinning slightly. Angrily, Felicia begins to roll down her window.

EXT. FELICIA'S HOUSE - NIGHT

Reaching down, Frank grabs the bulldog by its collar.

FRANK

Playing with Winston, huh?

With her window now rolled down all the

way, Felicia nervously tears into him, her fright still apparent.

FELICIA

You know, you're raising that dog the wrong way. You're making him much too territorial, too aggressive.

Still grinning, Frank is not taking her serious at all.

FRANK

Oh, my neighbor the vet.

Felicia pulls back her chin, narrowing her eyes.

FELICIA

You know, it's going to be a real shame if he ends up hurting somebody and he has to be put down because of your - your...

(can't find the right word)

Ughhhh!

Frank chuckles.

FRANK

What's the matter honey, cat got your tongue?

She looks at him, thinking quickly.

FELICIA
They say that all of a dog's virtues are his own and all of his vices are those of his master. Think about it.

Frank is about to say something back but Felicia quickly cuts him off.

FELICIA (CONT'D)
And try and show some responsibility and start cleaning up after him. He's defecating all over my lawn. My date stepped in a pile of his excrement this evening.

Grinning, Frank pats Winston upon his head.

FRANK
Good boy Winston.

Frustrated beyond belief, Felicia lets out a groan and drives off.

After a moment:

FRANK

Come on Winston, I got some rats I want you to take care of.

Winston BARKS.

EXT. VETERINARIAN OFFICE - NIGHT

Felicia's car, along with another car, are parked in the lot in front of the building. The lights are on inside.

INT. VETERINARIAN STORAGE HALL - NIGHT

Carrying a **SNOWY WHITE CAT**, which has one of its legs in a cast, Felicia is leading an obese woman, **MRS. MULLAN**, down a corridor.

The corridor is lined on one side by windows and on the other by cages built into the wall. The majority of these cages are empty save for a few which contain **DOGS** and **CATS**. They are joined in mid conversation.

MRS. MULLAN

I just can't thank you enough. I was worried to death. Are you sure she's going to be all right?

Exiting the hall, Felicia flicks off its lights.

INT. VETERINARIAN FRONT OFFICE - NIGHT

Moving out of the corridor, Felicia leads Mrs. Mullan into the front office.

FELICIA
Don't worry, she'll be fine. Just don't let her out of the house until this cast comes off.

Smiling, Felicia hands the cat to its owner who immediately starts to hug and cuddle it. The cat appears unusually alert, the way it is looking about is almost human-like.

MRS. MULLAN
Don't worry, I won't.
(to the cat)
Oh, Fluffy, my little baby, your little footsie-wootsie is hurt.
(to Felicia)
I honestly don't know what got into her. Usually, she never goes outside. I can't imagine why she was crossing that

highway next to the junkyard. It just doesn't make any sense.

Guiding Mrs. Mullan to the front door, Felicia glances up at the clock. It is almost midnight.

FELICIA

Well, just give her plenty of T.L.C.

MRS. MULLAN

Well that won't be any problem with this cat. She's so affectionate. She just wants to be near me all the time. Not like the other cats I've had. I know this is going to sound funny, but sometimes I could swear she's almost human.

Felicia smiles.

FELICIA

Yeah, I know. Every now and then you find a cat like that.

MRS. MULLAN
Well, thanks again...
Bye.

FELICIA
Bye.

Exiting through the front door, Mrs. Mullan leaves with her cat. Although now out of sight, she can be heard talking to her cat as she walks off.

MRS. MULLAN (O.S.)
Oh, poor little poopsie-woopsie. But don't you worry, mommy's going to take care of baby-wabby.

Smiling at what she is hearing, Felicia picks up her pocket book and is about to leave when she HEARS one of the cats from the adjacent corridor MEOW loudly.

Putting her pocket book down, she moves back into the corridor. The clock on the office wall reads one minute to midnight.

INT. STORAGE CORRIDOR - NIGHT

Not bothering to turn on the overhead lights, Felicia moves down the corridor and steps up to the cage containing the meowing cat.

The night's full moon can be seen clearly through the windows behind her and it is bathing the hall with its yellow glow.

FELICIA

Oh, what's wrong? You okay honey?

A dark **CAT** in an adjacent cage HISSES at the meowing cat. Sticking a paw through the vertical metal bars separating them, the aggressive cat scratches its meowing neighbor.

Opening the cage, Felicia gently yet quickly pulls the injured animal out. Holding it in her arms she begins to gently stroke it while scolding the other cat.

FELICIA

Oscar! Oh! I'm getting tired of your aggressiveness!

(to the injured cat)

Are you okay honey?

The moon behind her is very bright.

INT. VETERINARIAN FRONT OFFICE - NIGHT

The second hand is rhythmically jerking forward as the midnight hour approaches.

INT. STORAGE CORRIDOR - NIGHT

Examining the meowing cat with her fingers, Felicia finds the wound on the animal.

FELICIA
... This looks deep.

Spreading apart the cat's fur, she leans forward slightly to take a closer look at the wound.

FELICIA (CONT'D)
... Just hold still.

INT. VETERINARIAN FRONT OFFICE - NIGHT

The second hand continues to click forward. It is now only seconds away from midnight.

INT. STORAGE HALL - NIGHT

Gently reaching forward, with a probing finger, Felicia is about to touch the cat's wound.

INT. VETERINARIAN FRONT OFFICE - NIGHT

The second hand strikes the twelve. It is now MIDNIGHT.

INT. VETERINARIAN STORAGE HALL - NIGHT

Felicia's finger presses down upon the wound and the cat instinctively scratches her hand with its sharp claws. Dropping the cat, she grabs her hand in pain. It is bleeding. On the floor, the cat looks up at her and meows innocently.

FELICIA

Oh, I'm sorry... It's not your fault... oh...

Felicia wobbles upon her feet.

FELICIA

... I feel dizzy...

Steadying herself, she picks up the cat and gently places it into a cage a good distance away from Oscar. Leaning her back against the wall, she shakes her head in an attempt to clear it. She looks faint.

Staggering about, she moves down the

hall, keeping a hand against the wall to steady herself.

INT. VETERINARIAN FRONT OFFICE - NIGHT

Stepping into the front office, Felicia almost collapses, catching herself against a nearby counter. She cannot understand why she feels faint.

Picking up her pocket book she leaves, forgetting to turn off the lights and lock the door.

EXT. VETERINARIAN OFFICE - NIGHT

Feeling very groggy, Felicia starts towards her car. The night is silent and the clicking off her heels is all that can be heard. A moment passes.

FELICIA

(cat-like)

Meowwwww.

She stops and her eyes open wide. She has no idea why she just "Meowed." Confused, she continues towards and reaches her car.

INT. FELICIA'S CAR - NIGHT

Getting into the car, she blinks her eyes, having difficulty finding the right key on her ring. Finding the correct key, she inserts it into the ignition with a trembling hand.

Close on her eyes as they fill with worry and confusion. Leaning to one side, she looks into the rear view mirror. Shoots of blond hair are pushing their way up from every pore on her face. Gasping out in fright, she SCREAMS.

EXT. VETERINARIAN OFFICE - NIGHT

Felicia's scream ECHOES across the empty parking lot.

INT. FELICIA'S CAR - NIGHT

Hair is pushing up from all over Felicia's body. Shrinking, she is rapidly transforming into a cat.

Straining to look into the rear view mirror, she cannot believe what is happening to herself.

FELICIA

Oh my God... Oh, my God... what's happening to me?

Staring at her reflection, she sees long whiskers pushing out from her upper lips.

FELICIA

... I've got whiskers... Meowwww.

Looking about, she finds it hard to believe that the meow came from herself.

She meows again. This time much more cat-like.

FELICIA

(very cat-like)

Meowwww.

Continuing to transform and shrink, she is soon lost from sight, sinking into her clothing. There is a moment of silence.

FELICIA (V.O.)

Hey, how'd I get down here?

Looking about in confusion, she brings her paws up in front of her eyes. Immediately, her brow bunches up with confusion.

FELICIA (V.O.)
I'm ... I... I have paws!... I'm... I'm a cat. A cat!
(fast)
How can I be a cat?!
(a beat)
What am I going to do? What am I going to do?
(a beat)
Home... I've got to get home.

She looks up at the steering wheel.

FELICIA (V.O.)
Well, driving's out.
(a beat)
Oh God, I'm a cat! I don't believe this!

She looks up at the driver's side window which is opened.

FELICIA (V.O.)
Ah... well... Maybe I can...

Springing upwards, Felicia leaps through the window.

EXT. VETERINARIAN OFFICE - NIGHT

Landing down upon the pavement alongside of her car, Felicia sounds both surprised and happy that she successfully made the jump.

FELICIA (V.O.)
Ohhh, I... I made it!

Seeming more confident, Felicia giggles nervously.

FELICIA (V.O.) (CONT'D)
Th... That wasn't so bad... Hmmm, let's see now.

Twisting and turning her feline head, she looks about the parking lot.

FELICIA (V.O.) (CONT'D)
... Home... I... I've got to make it home.

Moving off across the lot, Felicia's back legs are moving in an uncoordinated manner. They do not seem to be moving in sync with her front legs.

FELICIA (V.O.)
... Four legs... I... I guess being a quadruped is going to take some getting used to.

Still unable to coordinate her rear and front limbs, Felicia nearly falls.

FELICIA (V.O.) (CONT'D)
God, this is harder than getting used to three inch heels.

Slowly, but surely, she begins to move her legs in sync. Within moments, she is moving in a fluid, graceful manner.

FELICIA (V.O.) (CONT'D)
Ah... oh... yeah, that's it. I - I think I've got it now... yeah... it's not so hard... Now to get home.

Act Two

EXT. FELICIA'S HOUSE - NIGHT

The house is dark except for a lit living room window. Off screen, the sounds of a late night TV program can be faintly heard.

INT. FELICIA'S LIVING ROOM - NIGHT

Curled up on her chair, Jeannie is watching late night TV. The popcorn bowl, resting in her lap, is now empty.

INT. JAN'S BEDROOM - NIGHT

Jan is resting peacefully in bed, sound asleep.

INT. CHRISTOPHER'S BEDROOM - NIGHT

Asleep in bed, Christopher is tossing and turning as if he is having a bad dream.

EXT. FOGGY FOREST - NIGHT (DREAM)

Rearing back its ugly head, the mother of all **WEREWOLVES** lets loose a blood curdling snarl. Screaming, Christopher tears off down a beaten path within a wooded hollow.

INT. CHRISTOPHER'S BEDROOM - NIGHT

Lying in bed, Christopher's elbows and knees are jerking about as if he is running in his sleep. His face is blanketed with fear.

EXT. FOGGY FOREST - NIGHT (DREAM)

Run, run, run. Christopher is running as fast as he can, fleeing from his beastly pursuer. The creature of the night, however, is gaining rapidly on the young boy and will soon overtake him.

Suddenly, Christopher finds that he is no longer running at full speed. Looking downwards, he is shocked to see that his legs are now moving in slow motion. Frantically swinging his elbows back and forth, he tries in desperation to increase his pace. It is no use. His legs are now moving slower than ever. Typical for a nightmare.

Glancing backwards, he is surprised to see that the werewolf is no longer pursuing him. In fact, the creature is nowhere to be seen. Confused, Christopher slows to a stop while still looking behind himself. Somewhat relieved, he turns back around.

Suddenly, his eyes bulge with terror and he screams. The werewolf, snarling angrily, is standing directly in front of him. Terrified, Christopher trips and falls. Rolling over on his back, he sees other **WEREWOLVES** slowly emerge from the surrounding forest and head towards him.

With their eyes blazing and saliva dripping from their sharp teeth, they slowly encircle him. He is going to be eaten alive by the most frightening looking werewolves ever seen. Surrounding him in every direction are hungry, beastly eyes.

Directly above him, the night's full moon bathes him with its eerie yellowish glow. He SCREAMS out.

INT. CHRISTOPHER'S BEDROOM - NIGHT

Jerking up into a seated position in bed, Christopher SCREAMS.

INT. LIVING ROOM - NIGHT

Hearing Christopher scream, Jeannie quickly leaps to her feet and runs up the stairs.

INT. HALLWAY - NIGHT

Bursting into the hall, Jeannie nearly collides with Jan who is also moving to investigate the scream. Both knowingly glance at one another and then rush towards Christopher's bedroom door.

INT. CHRISTOPHER'S BEDROOM - NIGHT

Jeannie and Jan enter the room and turn on the lights. Sitting up in bed, Christopher is breathing heavily and trembling.

JEANNIE

Honey, what's wrong?

CHRISTOPHER

Werewolves!

JEANNIE

What? Did you have a nightmare?

CHRISTOPHER

I... I couldn't run. My legs wouldn't go... Werewolves were chasing me.

Jan smiles as Jeannie sympathetically sits down besides Christopher.

JEANNIE
Oh, I'm sorry honey. I didn't mean to scare you with that full moon stuff.

JAN
What's the matter Christopher? Scared of a little werewolf?

CHRISTOPHER
Hey, you didn't see these werewolves.

JEANNIE
Okay now, cut it out.
(a beat/to Christopher)
Come on downstairs honey, I'll get you some milk and cookies. Then you can go back to bed.

CHRISTOPHER
Where's Mom? Is she home yet?

JEANNIE
No, but don't worry, she'll be home soon.

EXT. INTERSECTION - NIGHT

Felicia, still a cat, stops in front of an intersection. Several cars speed by.

FELICIA (V.O.)
Oh, no, gotta cross...
Don't want to end up like
Fluffy though... Got to
time this just right.

Looking left to right to left, she waits for an opening. Spotting one, she darts out across the avenue. A car that she did not see blares its horn, it is coming right at her. Screaming out, she freezes in place and covers her eyes with her paws.

Just missing her, the vehicle passes directly over her. Her scream echoes off the underside of the automobile.

Dropping her paws, she opens her eyes. Exhaling deeply, she looks at the departing vehicle.

FELICIA (V.O.)
Oh God, that was too
close.

Turning, her eyes bulge with terror.

Another car is heading straight towards her.

FELICIA (V.O.)

OH NO!!!

Taking off, she narrowly manages to avoid being hit as she leaps upon the opposite sidewalk.

FELICIA (V.O.)

(breathing heavily)

Oh God, I don't believe this. I almost ended up a road kill! ... How can this be happening?

Turning, she darts off and disappears into the night.

EXT. STREET - NIGHT

Trotting down the sidewalk, Felicia is heading towards her house which can be seen less than 100 yards in the distance.

FELICIA (V.O.)

Oh, almost there... "Home sweet home."

Moving closer and closer to home, she is now passing Frank's house.

FELICIA (V.O.)
How am I going to explain this to the kids? Forget that, how am I going to explain it at all? I... I can't even talk.

Off screen, a loud, brutal bark echoes through the darkness. Instantly, Felicia turns her head towards its source. It is Winston and he is barreling straight towards her with a full head of steam.

FELICIA (V.O.)
Oh my God!

Seeing that Winston has cut off safe passage to her home, Felicia takes off into her neighbor, Frank's, backyard.

EXT. FRANK'S BACKYARD - NIGHT

Winston is chasing Felicia around Frank's house. Screaming out, Felicia is diving through and about shrubbery in an attempt to lose the large canine. Round and round the backyard they go. Although monstrous, Winston is surprisingly fast and he is gaining on her. Glancing over her shoulder, Felicia sees this and screams even louder.

The back porch's light goes on and Frank steps out with a can of beer in hand. Seeing Winston chasing the cat brings a smile to his face.

FRANK

That's it Winston, get that cat! Damn things keep me up all night.

Spurned on by his master, Winston is almost upon Felicia. Spotting a small hole in the fence which separates her house from Frank's, she heads towards it. It is going to be close. Seeing this, Frank's smile disappears.

FRANK

Get it Winston! Don't let it get away!

Felicia has almost reached the hole. Taking flight, Winston leaps forward to pounce down upon her. Seeing this, she dives forward, disappearing into the hole in the fence. Bang! Winston's flat face slams against the fence. The hole is much too small for the bulldog to fit through. Felicia has gotten away.

FRANK

Damn!

EXT. FELICIA'S BACKYARD - NIGHT

Running away from the fence, Felicia stops to catch her breath.

FELICIA (V.O.)
Oh wow, oh wow, wow... That was too close. No wonder cats have nine lives, they need every one of them.

Having caught her breath, she turns and finds herself face to face with the large black cat from earlier. Startled, she gasps.

FELICIA (V.O.)
Okay, now what do you want?

Letting out a lust-filled, purring growl, the black cat begins to slowly circle her.

FELICIA (V.O.)
Uh-oh, I think I know. You're a boy cat, aren't you? And me, I'm a girl cat.
(a beat/nervous)
Time to get out of here.

Slowly backing up, Felicia attempts to move away from the black cat. It, however, follows her. Soon, she finds that she has backed into her house. She is cornered. There is nowhere else to go. Purring lustfully, the black cat slowly moves in on Felicia.

FELICIA (V.O.)
Oh no you don't... I don't plan on having kittens.

The black cat continues approaching.

FELICIA (V.O.) (CONT'D)
You... You just keep your distance. You... oh, I ... I feel strange.

Looking at her suspiciously, the black cat begins to back up. Felicia is growing. Within seconds, she is twice the size she was moments ago. Letting out a frightened hiss, the black cat turns and bolts off into the darkness.

FELICIA (V.O.)
Oh, I... I grew. But I... I'm still a cat. Just a bigger cat.

Looking up at her house, Felicia sees that one of Christopher's bedroom windows is open. There is a tree next to her from which, if climbed, she can jump to the window.

FELICIA (V.O.)
Christopher's window...
It's open.

Moving over to the tree, she starts to climb it.

INT. CHRISTOPHER'S BEDROOM - NIGHT

The door to Christopher's room opens. Standing in the hall with Christopher, Jeannie gently pushes the young boy into the room.

JEANNIE
You going to be okay now?

Nibbling on a cookie that he his holding, Christopher nods "Yes".

CHRISTOPHER
Yeah...

JEANNIE
Good. Well, hit the sack
kiddo.

She closes the door.

INT. HALLWAY - NIGHT

Closing the door, Jeannie moves down the hall and heads down the stairs.

EXT. SIDE OF THE HOUSE - NIGHT

Felicia, still a very large cat, is pulling herself up the tree. The moon above is bathing her in its bright yellow light. She starts to grow again.

FELICIA (V.O.)
Oh... I'm getting heavy... Feel dizzy.

Continuing to grow, she is transforming into a human-like cat creature.

INT. CHRISTOPHER'S BEDROOM - NIGHT

Lying in bed, Christopher glances about the room somewhat fearfully and then slowly closes his eyes.

EXT. CHRISTOPHER'S WINDOW - NIGHT

A feline, human sized hand drops down upon the window sill.

INT. CHRISTOPHER'S BEDROOM - NIGHT

Large cat-like hands start to pull up the screen in the bedroom's open window.

Christopher's eyes open and slowly swing towards the grinding sound. Something large, dark and furry (Felicia) drops into the room, falling in from the window. Hitting the floor, she vanishes from Christopher's sight, hidden by the corner of his bed.

The young boy's eyes bulge in terror and he slowly sits up in bed. Across the room he can see Felicia curled up in a ball on the floor. She is covered by dark shadows and the details of her cat-like appearance cannot be made out.

Christopher does not know what he is looking at. Groaning slightly, Felicia extends a clawed hand out towards him, moving her face out of the shadows. She is half human and half cat. It is impossible to recognize her as Felicia.

FELICIA

(cat-like raspy voice)

... Christopher...

Christopher's mouth drops open. He finds

that his voice is stolen by fear and he cannot scream. Unlike his dream, however, his legs work perfectly. Leaping off the bed, he runs out of the room, letting the door close behind himself.

INT. HALLWAY - NIGHT

Running down the hall, Christopher zooms into his sister's room.

INT. JAN'S BEDROOM - NIGHT

Leaping upon the bed, Christopher immediately awakens Jan from a sound sleep.

JAN

What? What's wrong?

Terrified, Christopher's mouth is moving but no words are coming out. Jan qrabs his shoulders in an attempt to calm him.

JAN

Relax, relax. Calm down.

Christopher tries to calm himself.

JAN

That's it. Just relax and take a deep breath.

Christopher takes a deep breath. He looks relaxed.

JAN

Okay, now tell me what's wrong.

Christopher's brow once again wrinkles up in fear and his mouth begins to move rapidly. Like before, he is unable to make a sound. Finally, after several comical moments of this, he finds his voice.

CHRISTOPHER

A werewolf... In my bedroom!

Immediately, Jan pulls her hands off his shoulders and looks at him disapprovingly.

JAN

Not werewolves again.

CHRISTOPHER

I'm serious. I swear there's a werewolf in my bedroom! It came in through the window.

She does not believe him.

CHRISTOPHER

Jan, I'm not kidding. Come on, let's go get Aunt Jeannie.

JAN

No, we're not going to bother her every time you have a bad dream.

(a beat/sighs)

Come on, I'll take you back to your room. Show you there's no werewolf there.

CHRISTOPHER

But Jan, it'll kill us!

JAN

(stern)

Come on.

Grabbing him by the hand, she pulls him out of the room and drags him into the hall. He is doing his best to fight against her.

INT. HALLWAY - NIGHT

Jan is pulling Christopher towards his closed bedroom door.

JAN

(whispering)

Stop it. I'm going to show you that there's no werewolf in there.

CHRISTOPHER

No Jan, it's going to kill us.

They reach the door and Jan spins around to face him. He is still struggling against her.

JAN

Stop it.

He stops his struggling.

JAN

Now let's go.

He leans back in his stance, preparing to resist her.

CHRISTOPHER

No way. I'm not getting torn apart. That thing'll rip my head off.

Jan rolls her eyes.

JAN

Okay, you stay out here
you baby.

She pulls open the door, preparing to step into the room.

CHRISTOPHER

No, Jan, please. Don't go
in there.

Ignoring her brother's pleas, she steps into the room, closing the door behind herself. Christopher backs up a step and stands motionless, listening.

Several tense, silent moments pass. His eyes widen as he sees his room's doorknob slowly begin to turn. He swallows in fear. Frozen in place, he just stands there as the door opens.

Standing in the doorway, Jan is holding Felicia who is now a regular sized cat again. Felicia looks groggy.

JAN

I found your werewolf.
Real big and scary huh?

Petting the cat, she turns her back to Christopher and steps back into the bedroom. Confused, Christopher follows her in.

INT. CHRISTOPHER'S BEDROOM - NIGHT

Turning on the lights, Jan sits down on the bed with her mother, the cat.

Christopher's eyes swing to where he had seen what he thought to be a werewolf. Looking about the room, he slowly moves over to his sister.

CHRISTOPHER
But... But there really was something ... 'Big" in here.

JAN
The only big thing in here is your imagination. It's only a cat. Hey, do you think Mom will let us keep it?

Snaking her head to clear it, Felicia jumps away from Jan. Landing on the bed, she turns to face her children and starts meowing. It looks as if she is trying to talk. It weird. Jan and Christopher exchange curious looks.

CHRISTOPHER
What... what's it doing?

JAN
I don't know...

Felicia stops meowing and tilts her head in disgust.

FELICIA (V.O.)
I - I can't talk, nothing but meows. Ohhh! What am I going to do?

Felicia starts to look about the room. The children are watching her do this. Her movements look human-like, not catlike.

CHRISTOPHER
This is a weird cat...

Felicia spots the Yatzee game which is still spilled out over the floor.

FELICIA (V.O.)
Yeah, Yatzee!

Jumping off the bed, Felicia runs over to the Yatzee game. Christopher smiles.

CHRISTOPHER

I think it wants to play Yatzee.

JAN

Don't be stupid, cats can't play Yatzee.

At this moment the cat, Felicia, starts to flip over the Yatzee spelling blocks with its paws in an unusually coordinated manner.

CHRISTOPHER

Oh yeah?

With the blocks, Felicia spells out: "IT IS ME"

JAN

(Reading blocks)

It is me?

The kids jump off the bed and shuffle up to the cat.

FELICIA (V.O.)

Okay, so far so good.

At once, Felicia starts flipping the blocks over with her paws, spelling out the word: "MOTHER" Jan reads the word aloud.

JAN
Mother?

The children do not understand.

CHRISTOPHER
How can a cat spell?

FELICIA (V.O.)
No, no, no, I'm not a cat.

Felicia starts rapidly flipping over the blocks again. She spells out: "NOT A CAT". Jan reads it aloud.

JAN
Not a cat...

Felicia continues flipping over the blocks, spelling out new words for them to read. Jan reads them aloud each time that they are spelled.

JAN
I am Mom.
(a beat)
I changed...
(a beat)
Into a cat.
(a beat)
It is me.

(a beat)
Mom...

FELICIA (V.O.)
Understand? It's me, Mom.

With her right paw, Felicia points at the word "MOM" and then at herself over and over again, trying to drive the point home. The kids are just looking at her with their mouths hanging open.

FELICIA (V.O.)
Ohh! ... They don't get it.

Rearranging the blocks, she quickly spells the name "JAN" and points to Jan. She then quickly spells the name "CHRISTOPHER" and points to her son.

The children are in shock. Spelling out the name "FELICIA" she points to herself. Flipping the blocks about, she spells out "I AM YOUR MOM" pointing to the blocks and then to herself. There is a moment of silence as the children stare at her in disbelief.

JAN
Mom?

FELICIA (V.O.)
Yes! Mom. Yes.

CHRISTOPHER
Mom? The cat's Mom?

Quickly flipping over the blocks, Felicia spells the word "YES".

JAN
Yes...

CHRISTOPHER
Oh wow... Neat.

FELICIA (V.O.)
Neat?

There is a flutter of wings from Jan's bedroom down the hall. Looking out the room's open door, Felicia can see the caged canary in the distant room.

FELICIA (V.O.)
Polly?
(cat-like)
A canary.
(aggressive)
A canary!

She takes off, running towards Jan's bedroom. Immediately, Jan and

Christopher chase after her.

JAN

Mom! Mom, where're you going?

INT. JAN'S BEDROOM - NIGHT

Bursting into the room, Felicia bounces off of the bed and crashes down upon the bird cage, knocking it to the floor. Striking the floor, the cage's door pops open and out flies Polly. Felicia starts to chase the canary about as Jan and Christopher race into the room.

JAN

Polly? Mom, what are you doing? - You're after Polly!

INT. LIVING ROOM - NIGHT

Sleeping upon the chair, Jeannie awakens as she hears the commotion upstairs. Quickly rising to her feet, she rushes towards the stairs.

INT. JAN'S BEDROOM - NIGHT

Jan and Christopher are chasing their mother who in turn is chasing Polly.

JAN

Mom, stop! Stop!

CHRISTOPHER

Mom, what are you doing?

Round and round the room they go as the mad chase continues. Rumbling down the hall, Jeannie bursts into the room.

JEANNIE

What's going on?

Felicia suddenly stops chasing Polly.

FELICIA (V.O.)

W... What am I doing? W - Why am I after Polly?

Quickly reaching down, Jan picks up Felicia, accidentally squeezing the air out of her.

JAN

Mom!

JEANNIE

What's that cat doing in here?

Jeannie spots the loose canary.

JEANNIE

It's trying to get your canary, huh?

As Jeannie moves towards Jan to take Felicia from her, Christopher speaks out.

CHRISTOPHER

No, it's not a cat. It's Mom. Mom. She changed into a cat.

Jeannie pulls the cat away from Jan and turns to address Christopher.

JEANNIE

You been dreaming again?

JAN

No, really Aunt Jeannie, it's Mom. She turned into a cat.

JEANNIE

What? What are you talking about?

SIMULTANEOUS DIALOGUE:

JAN

She spelled it to us with

the Yatzee blocks. The
cat's Mom.

CHRISTOPHER
The cat's Mom. She came through the window. She was really big and hairy but she changed into a cat.

SIMULTANEOUS DIALOGUE ENDS

JEANNIE
Look, I know you two want to keep the cat but you can't have a cat and a canary. They just don't mix.

JAN
But...

JEANNIE
(interrupting)
No buts.

Turning, Jeannie leaves the bedroom with the cat. Jan and Christopher immediately follow her.

INT. LIVING ROOM - NIGHT

Marching down the stairs with the cat, Jeannie is followed by her nephew and niece who are still pleading with her.

JAN

But Aunt Jeannie, it's not a cat. It really is Mom! She spelled with the blocks.

Reaching the base of the staircase, Jeannie moves to the front door.

CHRISTOPHER

Please Aunt Jeannie, listen to Jan. We're telling the truth.

Opening the door, Jeannie turns back to face the children.

JEANNIE

Sorry kids, I don't want to be mean but you can't keep the cat.

SIMULTANEOUS DIALOGUE:

JAN

But it's not a cat!

CHRISTOPHER
But it's not a cat!

SIMULTANEOUS DIALOGUE ENDS

Turning about, Jeannie tosses Felicia out the door.

EXT. FELICIA'S HOUSE - NIGHT

Thud, Felicia lands upon her derriere on the front walk. Swinging her head about, she sees the front door close behind her.

FELICIA (V.O.)
Argqhh! Jeannie, how could you be so stupid? Why didn't you listen to them?

INT. LIVING ROOM - NIGHT

JAN
You know, you just threw Mom out the front door!

JEANNIE
Don't be ridiculous. Your mom's out.

Noticing the time on the clock upon the

wall, Jeannie stops in mid sentence. It is almost two o'clock.

JEANNIE
Wow, it's late. Your mom's not back yet?

Confused, she moves to the phone.

JAN
She's back but she's a cat now. That's what we've been trying to tell you.

JEANNIE
Shhhh!

Picking up the phone, Jeannie starts to punch in a number. Frustrated, Jan and Christopher move to a window, looking outside for their mother.

EXT. FELICIA'S HOUSE - NIGHT

Felicia is still seated on the front walkway.

FELICIA (V .O.)
I can't believe I got thrown out of my own house.

Noticing her children in the window, Felicia begins waving at them with both her front paws.

FELICIA (V.O.)
Hey, hey, bring me back in. I'm sorry about Polly.

INT. LIVING ROOM - NIGHT

Seeing their mother, the kids begin to excitedly chatter to one another.

JAN
It's Mom, she's still outside.

CHRISTOPHER
We goota bring her back in.

On the phone, Jeannie covers her free ear with one hand as she hears the filtered sound of the other line beginning to ring.

EXT. VETERINARIAN OFFICE - NIGHT

The parking lot in front of the building is empty except for Felicia's car.

Off screen a telephone can be heard ringing.

INT. FRONT OFFICE - NIGHT

The office lights are still on. The phone is ringing.

EXT. FELICIA'S HOUSE - NIGHT

Felicia is continuing to frantically wave to her children who are looking out the window at her.

FELICIA (V.O.)
Oh, please, please, let me in. Open the door.

WINSTON'S P.O.V.: Breathing heavily, Winston is barreling across the lawn, heading straight towards Felicia.

BACK TO: Hearing the sound of something rapidly approaching her, Felicia turns and sees Winston racing towards her.

FELICIA (V.O.)
Oh no, not again!

Screaming, Felicia runs off with the bulldog in hot pursuit of her.

INT. LIVING ROOM - NIGHT

Screaming, Jan and Christopher turn towards their Aunt.

SIMULTANEOUS DIALOGUE:

JAN
The neighbor's dog is after Mom!

CHRISTOPHER
The bulldog's gonna eat Mom!

SIMULTANEOUS DIALOGUE ENDS

No one answering at Felicia's office, Jeannie hangs up the phone and turns to the children.

JAN
Mom's outside! The neighbor's dog is chasing her!

JEANNIE
What?

She quickly moves to the window and sees the bulldog chasing Felicia (as a cat) across their front lawn. As Jeannie watches the bulldog, she pulls out her cell phone and dials her sister's number with the single push of a button. It starts RINGING.

EXT. VETERINARIAN OFFICE - NIGHT

Felicia's car, in the parking lot: the cell phone in Felicia's purse in RINGING.

EXT. FELICIA'S HOUSE - NIGHT

Snorting loudly, the bulldog chases Felicia into Frank's yard. Felicia is still screaming.

INT. LIVING ROOM - NIGHT

Shaking her head, Jeannie pulls herself away from the window.

JEANNIE

Not that cat again.

Felicia's voicemail on her cell phone kicks in. Jeannie hangs up, growing more worried.

JAN

But Aunt Jeannie, Mom -

JEANNIE
(interrupting)
Put your shoes on. We're going to take a ride down to your mom's office to see what's taking her. I can't leave you kids alone.

The children immediately start up again but Jeannie quickly silences them.

JEANNIE
I don't 'want to hear it. Put your shoes on.

EXT. FRANK'S BACKYARD - NIGHT

Felicia is still screaming. The bulldog is gaining on her. A tree. She runs up it. Unable to follow her, Winston stands guard at the tree's base, looking up while barking angrily.

Frank's back porch light snaps on. He steps out of the house. Seeing that his dog has chased a cat up a tree, he lets a smile slowly curl up his face. In the tree, Felicia is trembling.

FELICIA (V.O.)
Oh no.

EXT. FELICIA'S HOUSE - NIGHT

The front door opens and Jeannie and the children step out of the house. Moving down the front walkway, they are heading towards Jeannie's car which is parked in the street. Their heads twisting and turning about, Jan and Christopher are looking for their mother while continuing to plead with their Aunt.

SIMULTANEOUS DIALOGUE:

JAN
Oh, please Auntie Jeannie, please. Let's go look for Mom, the dog's after her.

CHRISTOPHER
I can't see her anywhere. Maybe the dog got her.

SIMULTANEOUS DIALOGUE ENDS

Ignoring their pleas, Jeannie is moving straight towards her car.

EXT. FRANK'S BACKYARD - NIGHT

From her vantage point in the tree, Felicia can see her sister and her children moving towards Jeannie's car.

FELICIA (V.O.)
Wha... Where are you
going?

Looking down she sees Frank walking up to the tree. He has a malicious grin on his face. Winston is still barking loudly.

Felicia looks back out at the street in time to see her sister and her children getting into the car.

FELICIA (V.O.)
No.. . Don't leave me.
Don't.

FRANK
Good boy Winston. I'll
get the ladder.

Felicia swallows in fear.

FELICIA (V.O.)
The ladder?

She sees her sister's car drive off.

FELICIA (V.O.)
Oh no...

EXT. STREET - NIGHT

Jeannie's car is driving away. Jan and Christopher are looking back at their house.

INT. FRANK'S GARAGE - NIGHT

It is dark. One of the garage's doors opens. The full moon casts its glow inside and over a **DOZEN RATS** scurry out of sight.

Grinning, Frank steps into the doorway, holding Felicia suspended above the ground by the scruff of her neck. Her eyes are squinted in pain. Winston is at Frank's feet.

FELICIA (V.O.)
Oww! Ohh! What are you doing? My Neck. You're holding me by my neck!

FRANK
So we finally got one of you trespassing noise makers. You want to spend time on my property you're going to have to earn your keep.

Squinting, Frank looks about the dark garage, examining its nooks and crannies.

FRANK (CONT'D)
Winston wasn't fast enough but this should be right up your alley.

Tossing her into the garage, he chuckles.

FRANK
Get them rats.

Flipping head over heals, Felicia is flying through the air.

FELICIA (V.O.)
RATS?

She lands with a thump deep in the garage.

FRANK
When every last one of 'em is dead I'll let you out.

Winston barks and Frank slams the door shut. Felicia slowly rises to her feet, nervously looking about.

FELICIA (V.O.)
I'm... I'm trapped...

She hears some rats scurry about in the dark.

FELICIA (V.O.)
Trapped with rats...
Ohhh.. . This is the
worst night of my life.
(a beat)
Wait a minute... I - I
don't have to be scared,
not in here, I'm a cat.
They'll be scared of me.
Yeah. I don't have
anything to worry about.
Nothing at...

Her speech slows as she sees several **RATS** emerge from the darkness and slowly start to inch their way towards her.

FELICIA (V.O.)
A... I... I...
(a beat/confused)
Hey, what's the matter
with you. I'm a cat,
you're rats. Y... You
should be afraid of me.

Sensing Felicia's fear, other **RATS** begin

to emerge from the darkness and move towards her from all directions.

FELICIA (V.O.)
Uh oh.. . Maybe they know
I'm not a real cat.

Within moments, she is surrounded by a small army of large, dirty, greasy, grimy, smelly rats. Nervously staring at their hungry eyes, she sees them bear their long sharp teeth. This is too much for her and she screams out for help.

FELICIA (V.O.)
HELP! HELP! - SOMEBODY
HELP!

EXT. NEIGHBOR'S YARD BEHIND FRANK'S GARAGE - NIGHT

A good looking **BROWNISH-ORANGE CAT** stops dead in its tracks and reacts as if it can hear Felicia's screams and cries for help.

FELICIA (O.S.) (V.O.)
PLEASE, SOMEBODY HELP ME!
PLEASE!

Eyes widening, the cat takes off in the direction of her screams.

EXT. GARAGE - NIGHT

The brownish orange cat runs towards the back of the garage, leaping up towards one of its broken rear windows.

FELICIA (O.S.) (V.O.)
HELP! HELP!

INT. GARAGE - NIGHT

Landing upon a window sill in the back of the garage, the brownish orange cat peers in. He is just in time to see the army of rodents rushing towards Felicia. This cat is **TOM.**

TOM (V.O.)
Hey, leave her alone!

Turning, Felicia sees Tom leap through the broken window before him and rush to her aid.

FELICIA (V.O.)
What??

Leaping over the rats, Tom lands at Felicia's side. Standing upon his hind legs, he screeches out and the rodents take off. There is a clear path back to the broken window.

TOM (V.O.)
Come on, let's go.

Tom races off towards the window with Felicia following.

EXT. GARAGE - NIGHT

Tom and Felicia leap out of the window and land down upon the grass in the back of the garage.

TOM (V.O.)
I can't believe it. You're like me, aren't you?

FELICIA (V.O.)
I - I can hear your thoughts. Can you hear mine?

Tom nods "Yes". In the distance, they hear Winston barking. It sounds as if the dog is racing towards them.

FELICIA (V.O.)
Oh no, not that dog again.

TOM (V.O.)
Come on, follow me.

Both cats disappear into the darkness.

EXT. OLD HOUSE - NIGHT

Running up to an old house, Tom leads Felicia up onto its back porch where they stop to catch their breath.

TOM (V.O.)
We should be safe here.

FELICIA (V.O.)
You're not a regular cat, are you? You're a person like me.

TOM (V.O.)
So you really are a person. I thought I was the only one. How long have you been a cat?

FELICIA (V.O.)
How long? Well... A couple of hours. What about you?

TOM (V.O.)
Today... Today makes a month.

FELICIA (V.O.)
A month? H - How did it happen to you?

TOM (V.O.)
I don't know... I'm not sure. I remember feeling dizzy and then next thing I knew I was a cat. What about you?

FELICIA (V.O.)
(remembering)
Well... I was working late. I felt dizzy like you did... And then I changed.

TOM (V.O.)
That's it? Nothing else?

FELICIA (V.O.)
No, I don't - wait a minute. Right before I changed I was scratched by a cat.

Tom's eyebrows raise and his eyes widen.

TOM (V.O.)
Scratched by a cat? I was scratched by a cat too.

Right before I changed.
Do you think?

She thinks about it.

FELICIA (V.O.)
But... But how can that be? I've been scratched by cats plenty of times before. Never changed into a cat.

Tom lowers his head in thought.

TOM (V.O.)
Yeah... Same here.

Tom looks back up at her.

TOM (V.O.)
Well... maybe together we can get through this. My name's Tom. Tom Hansen, what's yours?

FELICIA (V.O.)
... Felicia Davenport.

TOM (V.O.)
Well, Felicia considering the circumstances...
(manages a chuckle)

It's very nice to meet
you.

He extends a paw to shake hands with her.

FELICIA (V.O.)

It's a relief to meet you
too.

Shaking his paw, she notices that he is bleeding from a cut on his arm.

FELICIA (V.O.)

Oh, you're bleeding. Are
you all right?

Tom turns his arm to look at the wound.

TOM (V.O.)

Hmm, I didn't even
notice... Must have
happened when we dove
through that window back
there.

FELICIA (V.O.)

Are you going to be okay?

TOM (V.O.)

Yeah, I think so. Nothing
compared to the mess
we're in.

FELICIA (V.O.)
Talking about messes, thanks for getting me out of that garage back there. That was very brave of you.

TOM (V.O.)
Oh, that was nothing. When you're with other animals you really have to ham it up or they'll sense that you're not a real cat and try to take advantage of you.

FELICIA (V.O.)
Oh...

There is a moment of silence between them.

FELICIA (V.O.)
What are we going to do now?

Tom starts looking around.

TOM (V.O.)
Well, before we do anything, I have to find a litter box, if you know

what I mean. Don't go
anywhere, I'll be right
back.

FELICIA (V.O.)
I'll wait right here.

He disappears into the darkness.

EXT. VETERINARIAN OFFICE - NIGHT

Jeannie's car pulls into the parking lot. The children are with her.

INT. JEANNIE'S CAR - NIGHT

Jeannie sees Felicia's car and notices that the lights are on inside her office.

JEANNIE
Looks like your mom's
still here. Wonder why
she didn't answer the
phone.

EXT. VETERINARIAN OFFICE - NIGHT

Jeannie's car parks alongside of Felicia's. They all get out. Heading towards the office, Jeannie happens to glance inside of Felicia's car and notices that the keys are in the ignition.

JEANNIE

She left her keys in the ignition. Guess she wants someone to steal her car.

Reaching into the car, she pulls out the keys and pockets them.

JEANNIE

Come on, let's go.

Jeannie heads towards the office with the kids.

INT. FRONT OFFICE - NIGHT

A key turns in the lock, the door opens. Jeannie and kids enter into the office. The lights are still on.

JEANNIE

(calling out)

Felicia?

(a beat/louder)

Felicia?

She steps into the dark hall.

INT. STORAGE HALL - NIGHT

Peering down the hall, Jeannie calls out for her sister.

JEANNIE
Felicia? Where are you?

There is no answer. She turns back towards the children.

INT. FRONT OFFICE - NIGHT

JEANNIE
Stay here, I'll be right back.

Jeannie disappears down the hall. Jan and Christopher look at each other with frustrated faces.

EXT. OLD HOUSE - NIGHT

Seated upon the porch, Felicia is impatiently awaiting Tom's return.

FELICIA (V.O.)
(to herself)
Come on Tom, what's taking you so long?

Hearing the porch door open, Felicia turns about to see her neighbor **GEORGE** step out of the house. Balding and sporting a beer belly, he appears to be in his late fifties. From her low vantage point he looks like a giant.

FELICIA (V.O.)
Uh oh.

Shuffling towards her, George smiles.

GEORGE
Hey, you're a nice little kitty. Where did you come from?

FELICIA (V.O.)
I... a...

Glancing over her shoulder, she looks off in the direction in which Tom disappeared.

FELICIA (V.O.)
(calling)
Tom... Oh, Tom.

She turns back around just as George gently scoops her up. She begins to squirm about.

FELICIA (V.O.)
Hey!

GEORGE
It's okay Kitty, I'm not going to hurt you. I bet you'd like a nice bowl of milk, wouldn't you?

Turning about, George heads back into the house with her. She keeps squirming about, trying to free herself.

FELICIA (V.O.)
Hey, what're you doing? Put me down. I - I don't drink milk, I'm lactose intolerant.

They disappear into the house together.

GEORGE (O.S.)
It's okay. You'll feel much better after a nice bowl of milk.

INT. FRONT OFFICE - NIGHT

Jeannie steps back into the office. She is confused.

JEANNIE

Your mom's not here. Car's out front, door's unlocked. But she's nowhere around.

JAN

Now are you going to listen to us? We told you, she's back home. That dog's chasing her.

JEANNIE

Oh, will you kids give up on that cat story.

Looking about the office, Jeannie is thinking concerned thoughts.

JEANNIE

Okay, let's get back in the car.

EXT. OLD HOUSE - NIGHT

Trotting out of the darkness, Tom heads towards the porch.

TOM (V.O.)

Sorry I took so lo...n...g

He sees that Felicia is not on the porch. He looks about for her.

TOM (V.O.)
(calling out)
Felicia?... Felicia? Where'd you go?

Through a lit kitchen window, Tom sees George holding Felicia. Bending, the man places her down upon the floor.

TOM (V.O.)
Oh no...

Tom runs up to the window.

INT. GEORGE'S KITCHEN - NIGHT

Tom is peering in through the window. Felicia is sitting upon the floor in front of a bowl of milk. Smiling, George is standing over her.

GEORGE
Go on kitty cat. Drink your milk.

Swinging her head about, Felicia is looking for an escape route. The room's door is closed.

FELICIA (V.O.)
Oh... How am I going to
get out of here?

GEORGE
What's the matter, don't
you like milk?

George's wife, **ELEANOR**, calls out from another room.

ELEANOR (O.S.)
(suspicious)
George, who's that? Who
are you talking to? You
don't have some young
girl in there, do you?

George rolls his eyes as if he has heard this a hundred times before.

GEORGE
No Eleanor, I don't have
"another woman" in here.
Just a cat.

ELEANOR (O.S.)
Are you lying to me?

Sighing, George looks down at Felicia.

GEORGE
Do you see what I have to put up with? That woman is going to drive me crazy.

ELEANOR (O.S.)
George?

GEORGE
Drink your milk little kitty, I'll be right back.

George leaves the room, closing the door on his way out.

GEORGE (O.S.)
No Eleanor, I'm not lying to you.

Tom knocks upon the window, drawing Felicia's attention. Seeing him, she jumps up upon the table in order to face him.

FELICIA (V.O.)
Tom.

TOM (V.O.)
What are you doing in there?

ELEANOR (O.S.)
How can I believe you when... When all you men are alike. All you have on your mind is one thing. One thing.

FELICIA (V.O.)
Never mind that. Just get me out of here... here... here... I - I feel dizzy...

GEORGE (O.S.)
How many times do I have to tell you that you're the only one for me?

Toppling off the table, Felicia falls to the floor.

TOM (V.O.)
Felicia? Felicia are you all right?

ELEANOR (O.S.)
D - Do you really mean that George?

GEORGE (O.S.)
Of course I mean it. Don't I tell you you are every day?

Tom's mouth drops open.

TOM (V.O.)
Oh no... You're going to change, aren't you?

INT. GEORGE'S LIVING ROOM - NIGHT

Eleanor is lean and in her early fifties.

ELEANOR
But... But I heard you talking to somebody.

GEORGE
It's a cat Eleanor. I was talking to a cat. Just a cat.

ELEANOR
But I -

GEORGE
(interrupting)
Wait here. I'll show it to you.

Walking away from his wife, George moves down a short hall, heading back towards the kitchen.

INT. SHORT HALL -NIGHT

GEORGE
Here Kitty Kitty...

Pulling open the kitchen door, George's eyes bulge and the word "Cat" sticks in his throat.

GEORGE
C...A ... T...

INT. GEORGE'S KITCHEN - NIGHT

Dazed, Felicia is seated upon the kitchen floor. Back in human form, she is stark naked.

GEORGE
Oh my God!

EXT. OLD HOUSE - NIGHT

Looking through the window, Tom's eyes are glued to Felicia's body. He finds her very attractive.

TOM (V.O.)
Oh my God.

INT. GEORGE'S KITCHEN - NIGHT

Coming to her senses, Felicia looks up at George, whose mouth is agape, and then back at her naked body.

Instantly, she wraps her arms around herself, covering her private parts.

FELICIA
Oh my God!

ELEANOR (O.S.)
George?

Now in a state of panic, George stumbles into the room and shuts the door behind himself. Looking about the kitchen, his mind begins to race.

GEORGE
Ah.... fast... fast...
ah... ah...

ELEANOR (O.S.)
Was that a woman's voice
I heard?

George swallows hard as he hears his wife heading towards the kitchen. Pulling Felicia to her feet, he quickly herds her over to a nearby closet.

GEORGE

In the closet... Hide in the closet.

Throwing open the closet door, George manages to get Felicia in just as his wife bursts into the room. Leaning his back against the now closed closet door, he forces himself to smile.

GEORGE

... Hi...

Eleanor suspiciously looks about the room.

ELEANOR

Where's your cat?

GEORGE

Ah... um... ah... um...

The closet door begins to rumble and shake as something is happening inside. Eleanor notices this. George swallows hard.

ELEANOR

Who's in that closet? You're hiding someone in that closet aren't you?

GEORGE
Ah... um... ah... um..

Eyes narrowed, Eleanor quickly moves up to George.

ELEANOR
You've got a girl in that closet, don't you?

GEORGE
Ah... um... ah... um...

EXT. OLD HOUSE - NIGHT

Tom is continuing to peer in through the window. Smiling, he is having a good time.

TOM (V.O.)
Now this is going to be good.

INT. GEORGE'S KITCHEN - NIGHT

Pushing George aside, Eleanor prepares to open the closet door.

ELEANOR
At last I've caught you.

GEORGE
Eleanor, it's not what you think! I swear I don't know where she came from.

Eleanor whips open the closet door.

ELEANOR
AH-HA! !

Felicia, once again a cat, races out of the closet, across the kitchen and out of it through the opened door to the living room. Unable to believe his eyes, George groans and then passes out.

EXT. OLD HOUSE - NIGHT

Having just witnessed Felicia run out of the kitchen, Tom leaps down from the window.

INT. GEORGE'S LIVING ROOM - NIGHT

Running through the living room, Felicia dives through an open window.

EXT. OLD HOUSE - NIGHT

Diving through the open window, Felicia lands next to Tom. Instantly, both cats run over to a nearby garage.

EXT. OLD GARAGE - NIGHT

Felicia leans up against the garage.

TOM (V.O.)
Are you all right?

Breathing heavily, Felicia nods her head.

FELICIA (V.O.)
Yeah but I'm a cat again. I turned back, all the way.

TOM (V.O.)
I know, it happens. My first night I kept turning back and forth. But then it stopped and I was just a cat. But it started again tonight. I changed back twice already. It only lasted for a couple of minutes though. I don't understand it.

FELICIA (V.O.)
Why... Why can't we

change back permanently?

Tom shrugs his shoulders.

TOM (V.O.)
I don't know.

There is a moment of silence.

TOM (V.O.)
A... by the way ... You looked really nice as a human.

FELICIA (V.O.)
Oh...

She is embarrassed.

FELICIA (V.O.) (CONT'D)
Thank you.

Looking into Felicia's eyes, Tom begins to purr. Felicia begins to feel a little uncomfortable.

FELICIA (V.O.)
Come... Come on, let's go this way. She walks off. Tom follows her.

EXT. FELICIA'S HOUSE - NIGHT

Car doors slam as Jeannie and the children disembark from her parked vehicle and march towards the house. The kid's heads are twisting and turning as they look for their mother.

CHRISTOPHER
(to Jan)
You see her?

JAN
No... But she's got to be around somewhere.

CHRISTOPHER
If the bulldog didn't get her...

EXT. A BACK YARD - NIGHT

Moving through the grass, Felicia lifts her chin, pointing her house out to Tom.

FELICIA (V.O.)
There... That's my house.

TOM (V.O.)
Do you think we'll be able to get in?

FELICIA (V.O.)
Getting in shouldn't be that hard. We just have to keep from getting thrown back out.

Turning together, they start off towards her house.

INT. LIVING ROOM - NIGHT

Picking up the phone, Jeannie is punching in a number as Jan and Christopher start to ascend the staircase.

JEANNIE
(to the kids)
Don't worry, we'll find out what happened to your mom. I'll be up in a little -
(into phone)
Hello, I'd like to report a missing person.

INT. HALL - NIGHT

Stepping into the hall, Jan and Christopher stop and turn to each other.

JAN

We're going to have to sneak outside and find Mom.

CHRISTOPHER

But Aunt Jeannie said -

JAN

(interrupting)

Aunt Jeannie doesn't believe us. It's up to us. Come on, we'll go out your window, down the tree.

Turning, the children move towards Christopher's room.

INT. LIVING ROOM - NIGHT

Jeannie is on the phone.

JEANNIE

What do you mean they have to be missing for 48 hours? That's the stupidest thing I ever heard. Let me talk to your supervisor.

(a beat)

Yeah, I'll hold.

EXT. A BACK YARD - NIGHT

Tom and Felicia are continuing towards Felicia's house. Stopping, she begins to shake her head. Feeling dizzy, she is losing her balance.

FELICIA (V.O.)
Oh no. ..

TOM (V.O.)
What? What's wrong?

FELICIA (V.O.)
I - I think I'm going to change again.

She drops to her knees.

EXT. FELICIA'S HOUSE - NIGHT

Climbing down the tree, the two children drop down to the ground. Jan swings her head about.

JAN
Come on, this way.

The two children run off toward the front.

EXT. A BACK YARD - NIGHT

Transforming, Felicia is becoming more and more human. Within seconds the transformation is completed. Breathing heavily, she sees that Tom is staring at her nakedness with a grin upon his face. Gasping, she covers herself with her arms.

FELICIA
Don't look!

Reaching forward, she quickly grabs Tom and spins him about.

TOM (V.O.)
Hey, careful.

Covering Tom's eyes with a hand, she quickly rises to her feet, her eyes nervously darting about.

TOM (V.O.)
Hey, what are you doing?

In her human form, Felicia can no longer hear Tom's thoughts.

FELICIA
Oh no... Naked! But...
But wait a minute. Maybe

I'll stay this way. No more cat.

A car pulls into the driveway behind her and lights up the surrounding area with its headlights. Letting out a startled cry, Felicia runs off towards her house, holding Tom blindfolded with a hand.

INT. LIVING ROOM - NIGHT

Jeannie is still on the phone, arguing.

JEANNIE

But... But this isn't like her, don't you understand? I'm telling you something happened to her ... What? I don't know what -

Jeannie stops in mid sentence as she sees, through the room's back windows, her sister running naked across the back yard holding a cat. With her mouth hanging open from shock, she slowly hangs up the phone while continuing to stare out the window.

EXT. FELICIA'S BACKYARD - NIGHT

Running with Tom, Felicia begins to

stagger, slowing her pace.

FELICIA
Oh no, it's not lasting.

TOM (V.O.)
You're changing again. I
feel funny... Uh oh.

Tom blinks his eyes.

The back door of Felicia's house opens and Jeannie rushes out. Spotting Felicia, she yells out.

JEANNIE
(yelling)
FELICIA!

Across the yard, Felicia is in a half human, half cat state. Losing her balance, she stumbles into the tall dense shrubbery in front of her and disappears from sight.

JEANNIE
Felicia?

Worried, Jeannie runs over to the shrubbery that her sister has disappeared behind. She stops in front of it.

JEANNIE

... Felicia?

The bushes shake but there is no verbal response. Reaching out with her hands, Jeannie spreads the shrubbery apart. Standing there, naked, is Tom in human form. Seen for the first time, he is a handsome man who is in his mid thirties. He looks groggy. Standing on the ground at his feet is Felicia who is once again a cat. Jeannie's mouth drops open. Looking downwards, she sees that Tom is naked. She screams. The scream pulls Tom out of his groggy state. Realizing that he is naked, his eyes bulge and he screams.

Jeannie lets out a second scream in response to his.

Bending down quickly, Tom scoops up Felicia and covers his private parts with her. She screams.

There is a split second of silence and then all three parties scream out once again, this time in unison.

Jeannie and Tom then take off, each running in a different direction. Jeannie back towards the house, Tom across the yard. Running off, Tom places Felicia behind himself, covering his naked buttocks with her.

FELICIA (V.O.)
Tom, Tom, couldn't you have at least covered my eyes?!

EXT. FELICIA'S HOUSE - NIGHT

Jan and Christopher are running towards their backyard.

EXT. SIDE OF FELICIA'S HOUSE - NIGHT

Running with Felicia held behind himself, Tom is rapidly transforming. He looks like a cross between a human and a cat. He stops as the two children appear directly in front of himself, having turned the corner.

Seeing him, the children stop and scream.

Tom screams pulling Felicia back around in front of himself. Felicia screams out again. Tom then takes off, sprinting towards the sidewalk as the two children flee towards the backyard.

EXT. STREET - NIGHT

Again holding Felicia behind himself, Tom is dashing down the sidewalk. In his half human form, his speed is incredible.

A moment passes.

FADE OUT

INT. LIVING ROOM - NIGHT

Jeannie and the children are stuffing large batteries into three different flashlights.

JEANNIE

Remember, if you see your mother yell out for me. Don't look at her... just yell out for me.

EXT. ALLEY - NIGHT

Tom and Felicia, both as cats, are slowly moving down a long alley. Noticing a long piece of string hanging from a garbage can that they are passing, Felicia instinctively begins to swat at it. After a number of swats, she realizes what she is doing.

FELICIA (V.O.)
W... What am I doing?

She stops.

TOM (V.O.)
I guess it comes with being a cat.

FELICIA (V.O.)
I guess so. Do you know I tried to kill my daughter's bird earlier tonight?

TOM (V.O.)
Yeah, the instincts are hard to control. Last week I played with a ball of yarn all night. I didn't realize what I was doing until I was too caught up in it to stop.

FELICIA (V.O.)
(thinking)
Like with Polly.

TOM (V.O.)
Those... Those were your kids I scared, weren't they?

Felicia smiles.

FELICIA (V.O.)
Yeah. Jan and Christopher.

TOM (V.O.)
So, you're married?

Felicia's smile drops.

FELICIA (V.O.)
No... Not any more. He died.

TOM (V.O.)
Sorry, I didn't know.

FELICIA (V.O.)
Oh, it's okay. It was years ago.

TOM (V.O.)
Oh.

FELICIA (V.O.)
What about you? Are you...

TOM (V.O.)
Married?

She nods yes.

TOM (V.O.)
No. Divorced, four years ago. No children.

FELICIA (V.O.)
Oh.
(a beat)
How come you're not remarried? After four years ... I mean...

She smiles and gives him back his line from earlier.

FELICIA (V.O.) (CONT'D)
You looked real nice as a human.

Tom is a little embarrassed.

TOM (V.O.)
You should have closed your eyes.

FELICIA (V.O.)
Like you closed yours?

Tom does not know what to say. There is a second or two of silence.

TOM (V.O.)
No, ah, I haven't remarried because, well because I guess I just haven't found the right person yet. What's your excuse?

FELICIA (V.O.)
I don't know. Same thing I guess.

There is a moment of silence as they look into each other's eyes. They are attracted to each other. Felicia turns her eyes away, looking down the alley.

FELICIA (V.O.)
Do... Do you think we're going to be cats forever?

TOM (V.O.)
I don't know. I was just about to give up hope before I met you. But there's got to be a way to turn back permanently.

FELICIA (V.O.)
God I hope so. I can't stand being a cat.

EARL (O.S. V.O.)
Hey don't knock it, it's
not that bad being a cat.

Shocked, they turn to see a scraggly, slick looking cat, **EARL**. He is seated upon a trash can to their left.

EARL (V.O. CONT'D)
In fact...
(he chuckles)
It's pretty damn good, "A
cat's life."

FELICIA (V.O.)
Wh... Who are you?

TOM (V.O.)
You're a person too...

EARL (V.O.)
Correction, was a person.
But that was five years
ago. Name's Earl.

Tom and Felicia glance at one another.

TOM (V.O.)
A... I'm Tom and ... and
this is Felicia.

EARL (V.O.)
Nice to meet you.

FELICIA (V.O.)
So you've been a cat for five years?

Earl nods "yes".

TOM (V.O.)
Before you changed ... Where you scratched by a cat like we were?

Earl grins.

EARL (V.O.)
Yup, that's what does the trick. Gotta get scratched by a cat. A real cat. And things have to be just right. We're talkin' full moon and the stroke of midnight.

TOM (V.O.)
A full moon?

FELICIA (V.O.)
The stroke of midnight?

EARL (V.O.)
Yup, there's gotta be a nice round moon and both hands gotta be on the twelve.

FELICIA (V.O.)
And that turns people into cats?

EARL (V.O.)
Sure does. Between that, spontaneous combustion and UFO abductions, you can account for just about all your missing people.

FELICIA (V.O.)
Well... is there any way to turn back?

EARL (V.O.)
And now why would you want to go and do a thing like that? Being a cat's the greatest.
(chuckles)
No stress, no worries, no rent to pay, no job! Just sleep and play. R and R.
(chuckles)

Can't beat that... Not even with a stick.

Tom and Felicia glance at each other.

FELICIA (V.O.)
(To Earl)
B... But we want to turn back. Oh.. . I - I'm feeling dizzy again.

TOM (V.O.)
Are you going to change again?

Felicia's dizzy spell leaves her.

FELICIA (V.O.)
No, I... I'm okay.

TOM (V.O.)
Are you sure?

EARL (V.O.)
Hey man, don't sweat it. It's just the pull of the full moon. Once a month it'll play around with you, changing you back and forth. Changes are just temporary though.

TOM (V.O.)
Is there a way to change
back permanently?

Thinking to himself, a sly smile curls up Earl's face. Hopping of his garbage can, he moves up to them.

EARL (V.O.)
There's a way. But before
I tell you, you gotta do
me a little favor.

FELICIA (V.O.)
Why?

EARL (V.O.)
'cause nothin' in this
world's free.
Everything's got a price.
You do me this favor and
I'll tell you how to
change back.

TOM (V.O.)
What's the favor?

EARL (V.O.)
I need you to give a
message to somebody for
me. She's a cat on the
other side of town.

Besides you two, she's
the only other "human"
cat I know. Sure, I knew
others but they all went
back like you want to.

FELICIA (V.O.)
How come you can't give
her the message?

EARL (V.O.)
Follow me, I'll show you.

Turning, he hops back up on his trash can. From there, he leaps onto a fire escape and begins to rapidly ascend it, heading towards the building's roof. Glancing at one another Tom and Felicia follow.

EXT. ROOF - NIGHT

The night's full moon is huge and it is bathing the entire roof top with its yellow glow. Moving to the roof's edge, Earl sits, waiting for Tom and Felicia. Walking up behind him, they stand at his sides, looking out over the city below.

EARL (V.O.)
See that big dark area
way over there?

Looking off, they see a large dark area in the distance which stands out in contrast to the lighted city surrounding it.

TOM (V.O.)
Yeah?

EARL (V.O.)
That's the junk yard. River's on its right, Highway's on its left, and she lives right behind it. 96 Cornwall. Only way to get there without drowning or getting hit is to go through the yard. And it's full of dogs. - Dobermans.

FELICIA (V.O.)
And you want us to go through there to give this message to her? What could be so important?

EARL (V.O.)
Hey, do you want to turn back into a human or not?

There is a moment of silence.

TOM (V.O.)
What's the message?

Earl grins.

EARL (V.O.)
Now that's more like it.
(a beat)
You're going to be giving the message to Susan. She's white and fluffy. In fact, that's what her owner calls her, Fluffy.

FELICIA (V.O.)
Fluffy?... Was she hit by a car tonight?

EARL (V.O.)
Yeah, she was trying to get to me. We're in love. And that's what this message is all about. I want you to tell her that we're gonna elope. As soon as she's all healed up I'm gonna chance another trip through the yard and sweep her off her paws. But it's important that you give her this message tonight.

(chuckles)
I don't want her to think
I forgot about her. What
do you say?

FELICIA (V.O.)
You won't tell us unless
we do this?

Earl smiles.

EARL (V.O.)
No way.

Tom and Felicia look at each other.

TOM (V.O.)
Okay... It's a deal.

EXT. FELICIA'S HOUSE - NIGHT

The full moon above is illuminating the homes below. There is no traffic on the street.

EXT. FELICIA'S BACK YARD - NIGHT

Holding flashlights, Jan and Christopher run up to their Aunt from across the yard. Using her flashlight, Jeannie is peering into the shrubbery surrounding Felicia's house.

JAN

We can't find her anywhere.

JEANNIE

She's not back there?

JAN

No. Maybe she's in the other neighbor's yard. The one with the bulldog.

Slowly, they all turns and look at the high fence that is separating their yard from Frank's.

EXT. FRANK'S BACK YARD - NIGHT

The fence is shaking. Jeannie pokes her head over it from the other side. Lifting her flashlight, she swings its beam around Frank's back yard. It is empty. No sign of either Felicia or Winston.

JAN (O.S.)

(whispering)

Do you see her?

JEANNIE

(whispering)

Shhh.

EXT. FELICIA'S BACK YARD - NIGHT

Peeking over the fence, Jeannie is standing on the backs of Jan and Christopher who are on their hands and knees. One of Jeannie's feet moves and a high heel digs into Christopher's spine.

CHRISTOPHER
(whispering)
Ow! Your shoe hurts!

She looks back at them.

JEANNIE
(whispering)
Sorry honey.

She looks back into Frank's yard.

JEANNIE
(Whispering)
Boost me up higher.

EXT. FRANK'S BACK YARD - NIGHT

Throwing her arms over the other side of the fence, Jeannie tries to pull herself over.

JEANNIE
(Whispering)
Higher... Push me higher.

EXT. FELICIA'S BACK YARD - NIGHT

Now on their feet, the children are straining to push Jeannie up over the fence.

CHRISTOPHER
(whispering)
She should go on a diet.

JEANNIE
(whispering)
I heard that.

Lifting a leg, Jeannie throws it on top of the fence.

EXT. FRANK'S BACK YARD - NIGHT

Balanced precariously on the top of the fence, Jeannie is thinking how to get over it without killing herself.

JEANNIE
(whispering)
Push my other leg up.

EXT. FELICIA'S BACK YARD - NIGHT

Straining, Jan and Christopher are pushing up Jeannie's other leg.

EXT. FRANK'S BACK YARD - NIGHT

Bringing her other leg up on top of the fence, Jeannie begins to swing her arms about in an attempt to balance herself. Her weight is shifting back and forth. It looks as if she is going to fall.

JEANNIE

Whoooo!

Trotting down the driveway, Winston stops as he sees Jeannie swinging about on the top of the fence. Snorting, he kicks his rear legs and takes off towards her.

Hearing the bulldog racing towards her, Jeannie turns her eyes to the dog. Slipping, she lets out a startled yell as she begins to topple off the fence. Twisting about on the way down, she manages to bend her knees and catch onto the top of the fence with her legs. She is now dangling upside down from the fence. Seeing Winston charging straight towards her, she lets out a frightened gasp.

JEANNIE

Ahh. Pull me up! Pull me up!

EXT. FELICIA'S BACK YARD - NIGHT

Jan is hopping up and down, trying to grab onto Jeannie's kicking feet which are dangling over the top of the fence.

JAN

Aunt Jeannie!

Finding a crack in the fence, Christopher peeks through it. He sees the bulldog racing towards Jeannie.

CHRISTOPHER

Oh no!

EXT. FRANK'S BACK YARD - NIGHT

Jumping up at Jeannie's dangling form, Winston bites into her long hair. Jeannie screams out. Sinking its teeth into her hair over and over again, the bulldog is chopping it down. Straining, Jeannie does a sit up.

EXT. FELICIA'S BACK YARD - NIGHT

Jeannie's face pops over the fence and she stretches out with her hands, reaching for Jan and Christopher.

JEANNIE

Help! Help! Pull me back!

Jumping up, they try to grab her hands but cannot.

EXT. FRANK'S BACK YARD - NIGHT

Unable to keep herself up in her sit up position, Jeannie drops back down, her hair falling within the bulldog's reach. Winston bites into it. She starts screaming out again.

EXT. FELICIA'S BACK YARD - NIGHT

Christopher is peeking through the crack.

CHRISTOPHER

The dog's going to eat her head!

JAN

Oh!

Thinking rapidly, she gets an idea.

JAN

Follow me.

Jan takes off, running towards the front yard. Christopher follows her.

EXT. FRANK'S BACK YARD - NIGHT

Jeannie's hair is being chewed down really short. Straining, she does a sit up again, grabbing onto the fence.

EXT. FELICIA'S BACKYARD - NIGHT

Jeannie's face appears. She sees that the children are nowhere in sight.

JEANNIE

Jan! Christopher!

Her hands slip and she drops back down, disappearing from sight.

EXT. FRANK'S BACK YARD - NIGHT

Running down the driveway, Jan and Christopher are charging the bulldog with their flashlights.

Pulling away a mouthful of Jeannie's hair, Winston turns to them. Barking, the dog charges them. Screaming out, they take off across Frank's yard.

Jeannie's legs lose their grip and she falls into the yard as Frank's porch light snaps on.

INT. FRANK'S PORCH - NIGHT

Looking out a window, Frank sees his dog chasing Jan and Christopher around his back yard.

FRANK

What the ...

EXT. FRANK'S BACK YARD - NIGHT

Running back towards the fence, the children race towards Jeannie. Jumping up, Jan and Christopher somehow manage to grab onto the top of the fence. Kicking wildly with their feet, they starts to pull themselves up it, leaving Jeannie to face the dog alone.

Turning to the fence, Jeannie leaps up, grabbing onto it. Kicking her legs frantically, she joins the children in their escape attempt.

Frank steps out onto his porch just as Jeannie and the two children all simultaneously flip over the fence.

EXT. FELICIA'S BACK YARD - NIGHT

Landing with a triple thump, Jeannie, Jan, and Christopher drops back into their yard. Winston is barking at them from the other side of the fence. Seeing that her pants are covered with her bitten off hair, Jeannie's mouth drops open.

JEANNIE
My hair... My poor hair...

Her face wrinkles up in anguish.

JEANNIE (CONT'D)
Ohh... I hate dogs.

EXT. JUNKYARD'S OUTER PERIMETER - NIGHT

Tom and Felicia step up to the junkyard's front gates. Stopping, they look at it fearfully. Surrounding the junkyard is a ten foot high wooden fence, topped by razor-wire. The front gate is composed of vertical iron bars.

TOM (V.O.)
Well, we're here. Are you sure you want to go through with this?

FELICIA (V.O.)
What choice do we have?
(a beat)

Do you see any of the dogs?

TOM (V.O.)
No, do you?

FELICIA (V.O.)
No.

Cautiously, they both move up to the yard's iron gates and peer in. Within, the junkyard is a seemingly endless sea of stacked, wrecked and crushed automobiles of every size, shape and make. There are no dogs in sight.

FELICIA (V.O.)
Wow, look how big it is.
(A beat)
But no dogs.

TOM (V.O.)
Maybe there aren't any.

Seemingly appearing out of nowhere, two **DOBERMAN PINSCHERS**, on the other side of the gate, pop up in front of them and start to bark loudly. Startled, Tom and Felicia leap back several feet. One by one, more dogs appear until there are a total of eight **DOBERMAN PINSCHERS**, all viciously barring their teeth.

FELICIA (V.O.)
No wonder Fluffy tried to take the highway.

TOM (V.O.)
Yeah...

There is a moment of silence.

FELICIA (V.O.)
How are we going to get through there?

Tom looks about.

TOM (V.O.)
Come on.

Tom trots off, moving away from the yard's front gates. Felicia follows him.

Soon, they are far enough away from the barking dogs that they can no longer see them and can barely hear them. Examining the fence, Tom spots a hole in its framework, near the base. It is big enough for them to crawl through.

TOM (V.O.)
I guess that's our way in.

FELICIA (V.O.)
You first.

TOM (V.O.)
Okay.

EXT. JUNKYARD - NIGHT

Cautiously popping his head out through the hole on the inside part of the fence, Tom looks about the junkyard. Finding that there are no dogs waiting, he crawls into the yard, followed by Felicia.

TOM (V.O.)
Okay, so far so good. Now to make it to the other side.

Tom starts off. Felicia's voice stops him.

FELICIA (V.O.)
Wh... What are we going to do, just walk across? The dogs'll see us.

TOM (V.O.)
Yeah... Well...

Looking about, he notices a thick cable, directly overhead, that runs across the junkyard. It just makes it over the fence on its way into the yard and can be reached from there.

TOM (V.O.)
Not if we're up there.

Felicia looks up at the cable.

FELICIA (V.O.)
Up there?

TOM (V.O.)
Yeah, come on. We're cats, remember? We can crawl across that wire easy. Right over this yard and we won't have to worry about the dogs at all.

Before Felicia can respond, Tom moves over to and up a pile of stacked cars near the fence.

From there, he can easily hop up onto the cable overhead. Although she is unsure if Tom's plan is sound, Felicia follows him anyway.

Jumping up onto the wire, Tom takes several steps forward. He is having no trouble balancing himself.

TOM (V.O.)
Yeah, this isn't going to be a problem at all. Piece of cake.

Having reached the top of the stack of cars, Felicia hops up onto the wire behind Tom. Swallowing nervously, she takes a few steps forward. Smiling, she is surprised by her cat-like coordination.

FELICIA (V.O.)
Yo... You're right Tom... This isn't so bad after all.

Moving forward, the cats head off over the yard.

EXT. JUNKYARD - NIGHT

Hearing something, a seated Doberman rises and looks overhead. Seeing Tom and Felicia, both in cat form, traversing the cable, the dog snarls and bares its teeth. Beginning to move, it keeps pace with the cats above.

UP ABOVE: Glancing down, Felicia notices the dog shadowing them.

FELICIA (V.O.)
Uh-oh, Tom we've got company.

TOM (V.O.)
Where?

FELICIA (V.O.)
Down there.

Tom glances down at the Doberman just as the other canines in the yard arrive and take part in shadowing him and Felicia. Staring up at him, the dogs are all growling softly. Tom chuckles.

FELICIA (V.O.) (CONT'D)
What are you laughing at?

TOM (V.O.)
Them.

He nods towards the angry dogs.

TOM (V.O.)
Hey don't worry, there's no way they can get us up here.
(a beat/chuckles again)
Look at them, they actually think that they're going to get us.

Not too bright, are they?

Relaxing a bit, Felicia manages to chuckle.

FELICIA (V.O.)
Yeah, I guess we are safe up here.
(a beat)
How much further?

TOM (V.O.)
Not too much, we're about halfway across now. It'll probably only take us... Uh-oh.

FELICIA (V.O.)
What... What's the matter?

Blinking his eyes, Tom is having trouble steadying himself upon the wire. He is losing his balance.

TOM (V.O.)
I... I'm dizzy.

Felicia's face floods with fear.

FELICIA (V.O.)
Oh no Tom... don't...

you... You can't change
up here... Not here.

Growing rapidly, Tom is changing into a human.

TOM (V.O.)
I... I can't help it!

DOWN BELOW: The dogs begin to bark as they see Tom transforming.

UP ABOVE: Continuing to rapidly transform, Tom's feet slip off the cable. Managing to grab a hand-hold on it, he is now dangling over the dogs. His weight is slowly beginning to pull the cable down. The frenzied dogs quickly gather in a circle directly below him, barring their saliva laced teeth.

FELICIA (V.O.)
Oh God Tom, hang on...
Hang on!

Tom, now completely transformed into a human, can no longer hear Felicia. Looking at the barking, growling dogs below, his eyes bulge.

TOM

Oh no!

Tom's weight is continuing to stretch the cable, dropping him lower and lower. The dogs begin to jump up, snapping at him.

TOM

Yikes! - N... N... Nice doggies, nice doggies ... D... Don't bite, don't bite ...

Swinging his legs upwards, Tom wraps his ankles around the cable in an effort to delay the inevitable. It is no use, he is continuing to sink down towards the dogs. Within seconds, they will be able to sink their teeth into him. Having dug her claws into the wire, Felicia is holding her position.

FELICIA (V.O.)

Tom no! Pull yourself up! Pull yourself up!

The dogs are within inches of Tom. Cringing, he closes his eyes. Suddenly, hair begins to sprout up from every pore on his body. Shrinking in size, he begins to rapidly transform back into a cat. As he grows lighter and lighter, the cable stops dropping and then begins to ascend higher and higher into the air. Feeling this, Tom opens his eyes.

TOM
(cat-like)
Yeah!

FELICIA (V.O.)
Oh Tom, thank God.

Almost a cat again, Tom's feet slip off of the rising cable. Hanging by his front paws, he turns his head to Felicia.

TOM (V.O.)
Help!

Quickly crawling forward, Felicia lowers a paw to help Tom.

FELICIA (V.O.)
Here, let me help you.

Her claws dig into one of his arms.

TOM (V.O.)
Ow! Hey, watch the claws.

Felicia pulls back her paw.

FELICIA (V.O.)
Oh, sorry.

TOM (V.O.)
Here, let me try...

Straining, he manages to pull himself up onto the cable. Breathing heavily, he looks down at the dogs which are now once again far below them.

TOM (V.O.)
Wow... That was close.

FELICIA (V.O.)
You can say that again.
(A beat)
Tom, I'm glad you're all right.

He is still looking down at the dogs.

TOM (V.O.)
Yeah... Me too.

Felicia smiles to herself, quickly putting on a serious face.

FELICIA (V.O.)
Tom, I feel dizzy.

Tom's eyes quickly swing to her.

TOM (V.O.)
What?!

Felicia smiles.

FELICIA (V.O.)
Just kidding.

Tom gives her a sour face which somewhat quickly turns into a smile.

TOM (V.O.)
Come-on, let's make it the rest of the way across.

FELICIA (V.O.)
Lead the way.

Turning, Tom starts off across the cable. Felicia follows him.

EXT. OTHER SIDE OF JUNK YARD - NIGHT

Crawling down the cable, Tom and Felicia step down onto the street and look left to right. There are a number of houses in front of them. The sign on the other side of the street reads: "CORNWALL"

TOM (V.O.)
Guess it's one of these.

FELICIA (V.O.)
Number 96 he said.

They cross the street, moving up onto the sidewalk.

EXT. SIDEWALK - NIGHT

Walking together, they look at the number on the house before them.

TOM (V.O.)
95.

FELICIA (V.O.)
Guess it's the next one.

TOM (V.O.)
Yeah.

They move to it.

EXT. SUSAN'S HOUSE - NIGHT

They step in front of Susan's house.

TOM (V.O.)
Yep, 96.

Felicia spots Susan (Fluffy) up on a second floor balcony. The cat is lying on a chair, asleep.

FELICIA (V.O.)
There she is.

Tom looks up. He sees that there is a tree in the yard which they can climb up to reach the balcony.

TOM (V.O.)
Guess we can climb the tree.

He moves his right shoulder about.

TOM (V.O.) (CONT'D)
Hope I can make it, shoulder's a little sore from hanging back there.

FELICIA (V.O.)
Oh, that's okay, I'll go. You can wait here.

TOM (V.O.)
You sure?

FELICIA (V.O.)
Yeah, no big deal.

TOM (V.O.)
Okay, I'll wait.

FELICIA (V.O.)
Be right back.

Scampering off, Felicia trots to the tree, quickly climbing up its trunk.

EXT. BALCONY - NIGHT

Climbing out on a limb, Felicia drops down upon the balcony, waking Susan.

SUSAN (V.O.)
Huh? Who?

FELICIA (V.O.)
It's okay, I'm Felicia. I have a message from Earl to give to you.

Susan's eyes light up.

SUSAN (V.O.)
Earl? What, what is it?

FELICIA (V.O.)
Well, he wanted me to tell you that as soon as your leg heals he wants to elope. He'll be coming to get you.

Susan is all smiles.

SUSAN (V.O.)
Oh, that Earl, he's so romantic. Tell him I'll be waiting.

Felicia smiles.

FELICIA (V.O.)
Okay. Well, nice meeting you. Bye.

SUSAN (V.O.)
Good-bye. And thanks for delivering the message.

Felicia nods, moving back towards the tree. A thought strikes her and she turns back to face Susan.

FELICIA (V.O.)
Susan... How come you're choosing to stay as a cat? Why don't you want to change back?

Susan does not answer right away.

SUSAN (V.O.)
Because I'm in love with Earl.
(a beat)
Earl, he loves being a

cat, and he doesn't want to change back. I guess I'd rather live with him in his world than be without him in mine.

FELICIA (V.O.)
Isn't that a lot to give up?

SUSAN (V.O.)
Love is a hard thing to find. I never found it as a human... somehow I managed to find it as a cat. I'm not going to take the chance of not finding it again. I'd rather stay like this.

FELICIA (V.O.)
I understand.

TOM (O.S. V.O.)
(calling)
Felicia?

Felicia and Susan look down at Tom.

FELICIA (V.O.)
Be down in a second.

She turns about to face Susan.

SUSAN (V.O.)
He's cute. You're planning on changing back?

Felicia nods "Yes".

SUSAN (V.O.)
And leave him behind? Maybe you should think twice.

FELICIA (V.O.)
Oh. no, he's changing too.

SUSAN (V.O.)
Oh. So when you're back are you and him? You know.

Felicia is caught off guard by this but she likes the idea.

FELICIA (V.O.)
Oh... Well... You never know.

EXT. SUSAN'S HOUSE - NIGHT

Waiting below, Tom is looking up at the porch. After a moment, he sees Felicia coming down the tree. Soon she is by his side.

TOM (V.O.)
All set?

FELICIA (V.O.)
Umhmm. How are we going to get back. Same way?

TOM (V.O.)
I was thinking about the river. Maybe there's a bank we can walk along.

FELICIA (V.O.)
Sounds like its worth a try. Can't be more dangerous than those dogs.

EXT. RIVER - NIGHT

Tom and Felicia are walking together up a river's bank. It is narrow and somewhat dangerous. The water alongside them is flowing swiftly.

FELICIA (V.O.)
Tom... I was thinking. When we get back, when this is all over, maybe you and I... Well, you know.

Tom looks into her eyes.

TOM (V.O.)
(eager)
What?

FELICIA (V.O.)
Well...

Lost in Tom's eyes, she takes a faulty step. Falling off the bank, she screams out as she splashes into the rapidly flowing river.

TOM (V.O.)
(yelling)
FELICIA!

Struggling to keep her head above the water, she is rapidly being pulled away.

FELICIA (V.O.)
(taking in mouth fulls of water)
Tom! ugh... Help! ugh... Help!

Tom begins to run down the bank, trying to keep up to her.

TOM (V.O.)
Felicia! Felicia!

It is no use, she is being pulled away too rapidly.

FELICIA (V.O.)
Tom!

Taking in a mouth full of water, she goes under. Throwing out his paws, Tom dives in to rescue her. Surfacing from the dive, Tom sees one of Felicia's outstretched paws slowly sink beneath the surface and disappear.

TOM (V.O.)
Oh no!

He dives under the surface.

EXT. UNDERWATER - NIGHT

Swimming underwater Tom sees Felicia's apparently lifeless form sinking downwards. He quickly swims towards her, pulling her to the surface.

EXT. RIVER - NIGHT

Pulling Felicia out of the river, Tom drags her up onto the bank. She is unconscious. He looks at her, unsure of what to do. Slowly leaning forward, he moves his mouth towards her. Her eyes flutter and open. She sees how close his face is to hers.

FELICIA (V.O.)
... Wha.. ?

TOM (V.O.)
I... I was going to try mouth to mouth.
(a beat)
Are you.. .

Under the full moon they kiss.

Meow

Act Three

INT. LIVING ROOM - NIGHT

Asleep on the couch, Christopher is lying next to Jan who is staring at the clock upon the wall. Standing, Jeannie is gazing into a hand-held mirror at her hair which has been dramatically shortened, compliments of Winston.

JAN

I wonder where Mom is?

Concerned, Jeannie lowers the mirror.

JEANNIE

... Me too.

EXT. ALLEY - NIGHT

Tom and Felicia are slowly walking up the alley. They are still wet from their ordeal in the river. Keeping close to one another, they are looking for Earl. Felicia spots him.

FELICIA (V.O.)

There he is.

Earl is resting comfortably in a cardboard box which is sandwiched between several garbage cans. Seeing them, he sits up in surprise.

EARL (V.O.)
Wow, I really didn't think you two were going to make it.

TOM (V.O.)
Well, we did.

Earl notices that they are wet.

EARL (V.O.)
Took the river back, huh? Pretty daring.

FELICIA (V.O.)
Yeah, I almost drowned. Now, we kept our end of the deal... How do we change back?

Pulling back his chin, Earl narrows his eyes suspiciously.

EARL (V.O.)
First, what color is her house?

TOM (V.O.)
Huh?

EARL (V.O.)
You heard me, what color's Susan's house.

Tom and Felicia glance at each other.

TOM (V.O.)
... White.

Earl chuckles.

EARL (V.O.)
Just testing. What did she say? You know, about eloping?

Despite her and Tom's circumstances, Felicia manages to smile.

FELICIA (V.O.)
She'll be waiting for you.

EARL (V.O.)
Great.
(a beat)
Okay, well never let it be said that Earl goes back on a deal. You want to change back right?

Looking at each other, they both nod "Yes."

EARL (V.O.)
Well, it's really simple

to do. All you gotta do
is get scratched by a
cat. A real cat, when the
moon's full.

He glances up at the moon.

EARL (V.O.) (CONT'D)
Like tonight. But you'd
better hurry, it'll be
daybreak soon and then
you'll have to wait
another month. But if you
want my advice, wait the
month. Maybe you'll
decide you don't want to
go back. This cat thing's
the most.

Felicia and Tom glance at each other.

TOM (V.O.)
No, we'd like to go back
tonight.

EARL (V.O.)
Well, to each his own.
Just go find a cat to
scratch you. Shouldn't be
too hard. You know, pick
a fight.

FELICIA (V.O.)
And we'll change back?
Permanently?

EARL (V.O.)
You got it.

FELICIA (V.O.)
Okay. Well, nice to have
met you.

EARL (V.O.)
Likewise.

Nodding to Earl, Tom turns with Felicia and they start to head off.

EARL (V.O.)
Oh, and by the way.

They turn back to him.

EARL (V.O.) (CONT'D)
After you turn back,
permanently, you won't
remember any of this. Not
a thing.

Tom and Felicia are shocked.

EARL (V.O.) (CONT'D)
Oh, you might remember

some of it tonight, if
you try real hard, but
once that sun comes up,
you're memory's wiped
clean forever.
(a beat/grins)
Still wanna change?

Unsure, they look at each other. Changing back will mean they will lose one another.

FELICIA (V.O.)
(to Tom)
I... I don't want to
forget you Tom... But,
I've got a family.

TOM (V.O.)
I... I understand.
(a beat)
Maybe if we change back
at the same time...

FELICIA (V.O.)
Maybe...

There is a moment of silence. Tom sighs.

TOM (V.O.)
Well, let's go pick a
fight.

FELICIA (V.O.)
(soft)
Okay...

Turning, they head off. Earl keeps his eyes on them as they leave.

EARL (V.O.)
Man... They should stay cats.

EXT. STREET - NIGHT

Walking down a city street, Tom and Felicia are slowly looking about.

TOM (V.O.)
I can't believe this. Six blocks and not one cat.
(a beat)
It's going to be dawn soon.

FELICIA (V.O.)
Maybe we won't be able to change tonight...

They are silent for a second. Each secretly hoping that they will not be able to turn back. Felicia's eyes suddenly widen as she sees a **TIGER STRIPPED CAT** to their left about to turn into a nearby alley.

FELICIA (V.O.)
L... Look.

Tom turns to see the cat disappear into the alley.

TOM (V.O.)
Well, we found one.
(a beat)
Guess we'd better follow it.

FELICIA (V.O.)
Yeah... I guess so.

INT. LONG ALLEY - NIGHT

The tiger stripped cat is slinking down the alley. Tom and Felicia appear behind it. Sensing their presence, it turns to face them, its eyes shimmering green in the darkness. Tom and Felicia stop.

FELICIA (V.O.)
(whispering)
Do you think it's a real cat?

TOM (V.O.)
(to cat)
Hey, are you real?

Not responding verbally, the cat continues to stare at them. Tom is a little disappointed.

TOM (V.O.)
Guess it's a real cat.
(a beat)
How do you want to do this?

FELICIA (V.O.)
I don't know... I guess just go up... and hit him.

Tom chuckles.

TOM (V.O.)
Just hit him?
(a beat)
Yeah, well I guess it'll work.

Lifting his chin, he shrugs his shoulders and inhales deeply.

TOM (V.O.)
Okay, let's go hit him.

Moving forward, Tom leads Felicia towards the awaiting cat. Hissing, the tiger stripped cat slowly begins backing away from them. As they get within several feet of the cat, it takes off, running down the alley.

TOM (V.O.)
I guess we chase him.

Felicia nods and they take off after the cat.

EXT. LONG ALLEY - NIGHT

Deep in the alley, the tiger stripped cat finds itself cornered. Moving upwards, it quickly climbs up on top of a giant open dumpster.

Running up to the dumpster, Tom and Felicia look up at the cat. Hanging low in the sky, the full moon is directly behind the feline. It hisses down at them.

TOM (V.O.)
I don't think we're going to have any trouble getting him to scratch us.
(a beat)
Follow me.

Tom starts climbing up the dumpster, Felicia follows him. Looking down at them, the hissing cat's hair raises up upon its back. Tom and Felicia reach the dumpster's top. It is open and its interior is deep and dark.

TOM (V.O.)
Careful...

Slowly, they move towards the tiger stripped act. It raises a paw, ready to defend itself. Its claws are sharp.

TOM (V.O.)
I think this is going to hurt.

FELICIA (V.O.)
Remember, let it scratch both of us. We have to change together.

Exhaling, Tom nods his head "Yes."

TOM (V.O.)
Okay... Move up closer.

She does so, almost walking at his side. Inching towards the cat, they ready themselves to be scratched. Making eye contact with Felicia, the cat swings at her, raking its claws down her arm. Screaming out in pain, she shifts her weight, accidentally bumping Tom and knocking him into the dumpster.

SIMULTANEOUS DIALOGUE:

FELICIA (V.O.)
(yelling)
TOM!

TOM (V.O.)
FELICCCIAAA!

INT. DUMPSTER - NIGHT

Tom drops into a pile of garbage down at the bottom of the deep dumpster. Groggy, he slowly rises to his feet.

EXT. LONG ALLEY - NIGHT

The cat scratches Felicia again, this time knocking her off the dumpster. She crashes down hard upon the alley floor. Letting out a screech, the tiger stripped cat leaps off the dumpster and bolts up the alley, disappearing into the direction from which it originally came. Lying on one side, Felicia moans as she tries to shake off her fall.

FELICIA (V.O.)
(groggy)
Tom?... Tom?...

INT. DUMPSTER - NIGHT

Tom is attempting to get out of the dumpster but its walls are too sheer and too high.

TOM (V.O.)
Felicia!... Felicia! ...

EXT. LONG ALLEY - NIGHT

Bathed in the moonlight from above, Felicia begins to rapidly transform back into a human.

FELICIA (V.O.)
Oh no. Tom!

INT. DUMPSTER - NIGHT

Tom is springing up and down, trying to get out of the dumpster. It is an impossible feat.

EXT. LONG ALLEY - NIGHT

Felicia is half human, half cat.

TOM (O.S.) (V.O.)
Felicia! ...

FELICIA
(cat-like)
Tooommm!

Continuing to transform, she collapses to the cold pavement beneath her.

INT. DUMPSTER - NIGHT

Tiring, Tom is not jumping as high. He stops jumping and listens.

TOM (V.O.)
Felicia?

EXT. LONG ALLEY - NIGHT

Felicia is once again a human. She can no longer hear Tom's thoughts. Groggy, she lifts her face and looks around at hersurroundings. She is confused.

TOM (V.O.)
Felicia, did you change?... Felicia? Felicia!

FELICIA
Wha... Where am I? H...

How'd I get here?

Noticing that she is naked, her eyes nervously dart about the alley. Seeing an old blanket in the trash, she grabs it and wraps it around herself.

TOM (V.O.)
Felicia... You... You changed ... Didn't you? ... You can't hear me anymore... Can you?

Trembling slightly, Felicia rises to her feet.

FELICIA
Home... I've got to get home.

Turning her back to the dumpster, she starts to stumble off.

INT. DUMPSTER - NIGHT

Hearing the piddle-paddle of bare feet, Tom becomes silent. Cocking his head, he listens.

EXT. LONG ALLEY - NIGHT

Felicia is moving further and further away from the dumpster.

TOM (O.S.) (V.O.)
Felicia... Don't... Don't forget me.

Felicia is continuing to move off. The dumpster is soon lost from sight.

TOM (O.S.) (V.O.)(CONT'D)
(voice trailing away)
Don't leave me.

INT. LIVING ROOM - NIGHT

Jeannie and the kids are sleeping upon the couch. After a moment of silence, they hear somebody rapping on the front door. Rising to her feet, Jeannie cautiously moves towards the door. Wide-eyed, the children watch her.

JEANNIE
Who is it?

FELICIA (O.S.)
(sounds shaken up)
It... It's me, Felicia.

Leaping to their feet, the children join Jeannie, running to the door.

SIMULTANEOUS DIALOGUE:

JAN
Mom... mom, you're back!

CHRISTOPHER
Mom!... Mom!

SIMULTANEOUS DIALOGUE ENDS

Smiling, Jeannie opens the door. Seeing her sister's condition, her mouth drops open in shock as does Jan's and Christopher's. Putting an arm around her sister, Jeannie quickly pulls Felicia into the house and shuts the door.

JEANNIE
Oh my God! Felicia, what happened to you?

FELICIA
(still disoriented)
I... I don't know... I can't remember anything. Nothing at all. ..

JEANNIE
Did that naked man do this to you?

FELICIA
Naked man? What naked man?

JEANNIE

The one you were running around with in the back yard!

FELICIA

In the back yard?

CHRISTOPHER

Yeah, the one that was changing into a werewolf!

FELICIA

Werewolf?

JAN

Mom, you don't remember being a cat?

FELICIA

A cat?

Still disoriented from her ordeal. Felicia stumbles forward and rubs her temples.

JEANNIE

(very concerned)

Felicia, I'm going to take you down to the emergency room. Have them look at you.

FELICIA

No... No, just... Just let me take a hot shower... Get some clothes on.

Thinking, Jeannie looks at her for a moment.

JEANNIE

Okay, I'll make some coffee. When you come down we'll try and figure out what happened to you.

Felicia nods.

JEANNIE

Sure you're going to be all right?

Felicia nods again. Turning, she moves towards the staircase. Suddenly, a thought strikes her and she turns back towards her sister.

FELICIA

Did you do something with your hair?

The children smile.

CHRISTOPHER

The bulldog gave her a haircut.

FELICIA

What?

Recalling her ordeal with the dog, Jeannie grimaces.

JEANNIE

I'll tell you about it later. Just go and take your shower.

Nodding, Felicia turns and moves up the staircase.

INT. BATHROOM - NIGHT

Standing in the bathroom, Felicia reaches behind the bathtub's curtain and turns on the shower. Steam begins to fill the room. Holding herself motionless for a moment or two, Felicia becomes lost in thought.

FELICIA

... A cat?...

INT. KITCHEN - NIGHT

Jeannie is making coffee. The two children are sitting at the table.

JEANNIE

Look kids, your mom's been through a lot tonight. I don't want you bringing this cat stuff up again. Take it easy on her.

INT. BATHROOM - NIGHT

In the shower, Felicia is soaping up. Noticing the cat scratches on her right arm, she becomes motionless. She looks confused and disturbed.

INT. KITCHEN - NIGHT

Dressed in a bathrobe, Felicia steps into the kitchen. Jeannie cannot help but notice the confused, empty look upon her face.

JEANNIE

Are you sure you're all right?

Moving over to the table, Felicia sits down.

FELICIA

I... I don't know. I feel as if there's something I should remember... Something important.

Jeannie sits down across from her.

JEANNIE

Well, try to remember.

Felicia tries but she cannot. After a moment, she shakes her head in frustration.

FELICIA

I... I can't.

JAN

Mom, don't you remember spelling with the blocks?

FELICIA

The blocks?

JEANNIE

Jan!

JAN

(ignoring Jeannie)

Mom, don't you remember the blocks?

Felicia spills her coffee and her face goes blank. She has a flashback.

INT. CHRISTOPHER'S ROOM - NIGHT (FLASHBACK)

FELICIA'S P.O.V.: Reaching down with her paws, Felicia is flipping over the Yatzee blocks. She spells the words "INTO A CAT".

INT. KITCHEN - NIGHT

JEANNIE
Felicia?

Staring straight ahead, Felicia's mind is a million miles away.

EXT. FRANK'S BACK YARD - NIGHT (FLASHBACK)

FELICIA'S P.O.V.: From up in the tree, she sees Frank grinning up at her. Winston can be heard barking.

FRANK
Good boy Winston. I'll get the ladder.

INT. GARAGE - NIGHT (FLASHBACK)

FELICIA'S P.O.V.: Tom is upon the sill of the broken window in the back of the garage.

TOM (V.O.)
Hey, leave her alone!

EXT. OLD HOUSE - NIGHT (FLASHBACK)

FELICIA'S P.O.V.: She sees George, smiling, shuffling towards her.

GEORGE
Hey, you're a nice little kitty. Where did you come from?

INT. KITCHEN - NIGHT

JEANNIE
Felicia, what's wrong?

Staring blankly ahead, Felicia waves a hand to silence Jeannie.

EXT. ALLEY - NIGHT (FLASHBACK)

FELICIA'S P.O.V.:

TOM (V.O.)
Is there a way to change back permanently?

EARL (V.O.)
There's a way. But before I tell you, you gotta do me a little favor.

EXT. JUNKYARD - NIGHT (FLASHBACK)

FELICIA'S P.O.V.: In human form, Tom has his ankles wrapped around the cable which is slowly sinking down towards the barking dogs bellow.

FELICIA (V.O.)
Tom no! Pull yourself up! Pull yourself up!

EXT. BALCONY - NIGHT (FLASHBACK)

FELICIA'S P.O.V.: She is talking to Susan on the balcony.

SUSAN (V.O.)
And leave him behind?
Maybe you should think
twice.

FELICIA (V.O.)
Oh no, he's changing too.

EXT. RIVER - NIGHT (FLASHBACK)

FELICIA'S P.O.V.: Tom's face is close to hers.

TOM (V.O.)
I... I was going to try
mouth to mouth.
(a beat)
Are you...

They kiss.

EXT. ALLEY - NIGHT (FLASHBACK)

FELICIA'S P.O.V.:

EARL (V.O.)
All you gotta do is get
scratched by a cat. A
real cat.

EXT. ALLEY - NIGHT
(FLASHBACK)

FELICIA'S P.O.V.:

EARL (V.O.)
You won't remember any of this. Not a thing.

Felicia hears Earl's last line several more times.

EARL (V.O.) (CONT'D)
(a beat)
Not a thing.
(a beat)
Not a thing.
(a beat)
Not a thing.

EXT. LONG ALLEY - NIGHT
(FLASHBACK)

FELICIA'S P.O.V.: The tiger stripped cat scratches her. Bumping Tom, she accidentally sends him falling into the dumpster.

SIMULTANEOUS DIALOGUE:

FELICIA (V.O.)
(yelling)
TOM!

TOM (V.O.)
(yelling)
FELICCCIAAAA!

EXT. LONG ALLEY - NIGHT (FLASHBACK)

FELICIA'S P.O.V.: Felicia is staring at the dumpster from ground level.

TOM (V.O.)
... Felicia?...

FELICIA
(cat-like)
Tooommm!

INT. KITCHEN - NIGHT

Snapping out of her flashbacks, Felicia springs to her feet.

FELICIA
Tom! Oh my God, I remember... I remember it all!

JAN
(excited)
Mom, you remember!

FELICIA
(excited)
Yes, I was a cat!

Turning to her confused sister, Felicia grabs her by her shoulders and begins shaking her.

FELICIA (CONT'D)
I WAS A CAT!

CHRISTOPHER
Yeah!

Quickly whipping her head about, she looks out of the window. Although it is still dark outside, the full moon is beginning to hang low in the horizon. Daybreak is coming.

FELICIA
Oh my God, it's going to be light soon.

Running away from the table, she dashes towards the living room.

FELICIA (CONT'D)
(as she runs)
Fast, fast put your shoes on. We gotta get Tom!

INT. LIVING ROOM - NIGHT

Jeannie, Jan and Christopher run into the living room, following Felicia. Jeannie does not know what is going on.

JEANNIE

Tom? Who's Tom, that naked guy?

EXT. FELICIA'S HOUSE - NIGHT

With their shoes on, they are all sprinting towards Jeannie's car. Felicia is still wearing her bathrobe.

JEANNIE

This is crazy, what are we doing? I really think you need a doctor.

FELICIA

(frantic)

Trust me. Just trust me.

They are all about to get into the car.

FRANK (O.S.)

Hold it!

Turning, they see that Frank is angrily standing behind them with his bulldog at his side. Winston is softly growling.

FRANK (CONT'D)
You people've been trespassing over my property all night and you're not going to get away with it!

FELICIA
(ignoring Frank)
In the car.

They all begin to pile into the car. Lunging forward, Frank grabs Felicia by her arm, stopping her.

FRANK
You're not going anywhere.

Felicia angrily turns towards him.

FELICIA
Take your hand off of me, you... you... You locked me up in your garage with your Rats!!

Boom! She lashes out and punches him right in his nose, knocking him down to the sidewalk.

The kids cheer. The bulldog barks.

Jeannie angrily turns towards the canine.

JEANNIE
(screams/to Winston)
GET OUT OF HERE!!

Tucking tail, Winston takes off whimpering. Again, the kids cheer.

FELICIA
(frantic/urgent)
Quick, into the car.

INT. JEANNIE'S CAR - NIGHT

Doors slam shut as they all pile into the car. Jeannie is in the driver's seat.

FELICIA
Go, go, we don't have much time. When the sun comes up I'm going to forget it all!

EXT. STREET - NIGHT

Jeannie's car speeds off.

EXT. STREET - NIGHT

Having just emptied a dumpster, a monstrous garbage truck lowers it back down to the pavement. It lands with a heavy thud. Gears grind and inside the truck the collected garbage is squashed and compacted. Moving off, the truck turns into a long alley.

EXT. LONG ALLEY - NIGHT

The monstrous truck begins to rumble down the alley. Dirty, black smoke is pouring out of its tailpipe.

INT. DUMPSTER - NIGHT

Having given up hope of climbing out of the dumpster, Tom is seated in the trash. He hears the truck approaching in the distance.

EXT. LONG ALLEY - NIGHT

Slowly, the garbage truck is moving towards the dumpster that Tom is trapped within.

INT. DUMPSTER - NIGHT

Hearing the monstrous truck's brakes squealing as it comes to a stop, Tom tilts his head and rises to his four legs.

TOM (V.O.)
Huh?

EXT. LONG ALLEY - NIGHT

Cold, hard steel arms reach out towards the dumpster.

INT. DUMPSTER - NIGHT

The dumpster rocks as the truck's arms grab it. Metal groaning against metal.

TOM (V.O.)
Uh oh.

The dumpster lurches as it slowly begins to rise upwards.

EXT. LONG ALLEY - NIGHT

The garbage truck is lifting the dumpster up into the air, preparing to swallow its contents.

EXT. STREET - NIGHT

Jeannie's car is rapidly moving down the street. The long alley is up ahead of it.

INT. JEANNIE'S CAR - NIGHT

Seeing the alley up ahead of them, Felicia points it out to her sister.

FELICIA
There, turn there.

JEANNIE
Into the alley?

FELICIA
Yes.

INT. DUMPSTER - NIGHT

Tom is sliding, along with the trash, down the tilting dumpster's floor.

EXT. LONG ALLEY - NIGHT

Continuing to rise above the truck, the dumpster is about to have its contents poured into the turning gears within the top of the monstrous vehicle.

EXT. STREET - NIGHT

Jeannie's car turns into the alley.

INT. JEANNIE'S CAR - NIGHT

Turning into the alley, Felicia's eyes bulge as she sees the garbage truck about to empty the dumpster.

FELICIA

Oh my God!

Quickly reaching over, she begins to beep the car's horn.

FELICIA (CONT'D)

Fast, pull up to that truck.

EXT. LONG ALLEY - NIGHT

Trash begins to pour out of the dumpster. Landing within the opening on the top of the truck, it is instantly ground up and compacted.

INT. DUMPSTER - NIGHT

Tom is all the way in the back of the dumpster, trying to dig his claws into its metal floor. It is no use, he is sliding forward with the rest of the trash. Seeing the grinding gears within the truck, he yells out in horror.

EXT. LONG ALLEY - NIGHT

Jeannie's car screeches up and stops alongside the garbage truck. Leaping out of the automobile, Felicia runs up to and begins to pound upon the truck's driver's side door.

FELICIA
Stop! Stop! Stop!

INT. DUMPSTER - NIGHT

Tom tumbles out of the dumpster.

FELICIA (O.S.)
Stop this truck!

EXT. LONG ALLEY - NIGHT

On the top of the truck: Somehow, Tom manages to grab onto the lip of the dumpster with one of his paws. Dangling above the jaws of death, he is yelling out in horror.

On the side of the truck: Felicia is still banging on the driver's side door.

FELICIA

Stop! Stop the truck!
Stop!

On the top of the truck: Tom slips, falling downwards towards a certain death.

Below, Felicia sees this and gasps. Suddenly, their is a loud clunking sound and the truck's grinding gears stop. Tom lands upon the garbage covered gears with a thump.

On the side of the truck: Seeing the driver's window roll down, Felicia stops her banging and yelling. A burly **DRIVER** angrily looks out at her.

DRIVER

Hey lady, what's your
problem?!

FELICIA

There... There's a cat in
that dumpster!

At once, she crawls up on top of the truck.

DRIVER

Lady, what are you doing?

On top of the truck: Felicia crawls forward on her stomach and looks down into the compactor. She sees Tom sitting there, breathing heavily.

FELICIA

TOM!

TOM (V.O.)

Felicia! You remembered.

She stretches her arms down into the compactor. Rising up on his hind legs, Tom reaches his front paws up to her. She grabs them, pulling him to safety.

FELICIA

Tom...

Suddenly realizing her predicament, she looks up at the brightening sky.

FELICIA

We... We have to find a cat to scratch you.

(a beat/thinking)

Oscar! At my office!

EXT. VETERINARIAN OFFICE - ALMOST DAWN

Jeannie's car jerks forward as it screeches to a stop in front of the office. The full moon is slowly disappearing in the brightening sky.

They all get out of the vehicle. Felicia is holding Tom. At once, she sprints towards the building's front door, followed by Jeannie and the children.

JEANNIE
This is all crazy. I can't believe I'm actually going along with this.

Before Felicia steps into the front door, she glances up into the sky.

FELICIA
Oh, the moon's almost gone.

TOM (V.O.)
We're not going to make it. I'm trapped as a cat.

INT. FRONT OFFICE - ALMOST DAWN

Rushing through the front office, Felicia runs into the corridor which houses the caged animals. Her children are right behind her. Jeannie is behind them.

INT. STORAGE HALL - ALMOST DAWN TO DAWN TRANSITION

Running down the corridor, Felicia slides to a stop in front of the cage containing Oscar, the aggressive cat. It hisses angrily.

FELICIA
I'm sorry Tom, this is going to hurt.

Although Tom knows Felicia cannot hear him, he is continuing to speak.

TOM (V.O.)
Do it. Just do it! Throw me in.

Felicia opens the cage. The cat within continues to hiss aggressively. Tom closes his eyes. She throws him in. Tom begins to scream as the cat begins to rake its claws all over his body.

FELICIA
(to Jan)
Get a blanket.

Jan runs off to do so.

JEANNIE

What are you doing to that poor cat? You've flipped!

Her eyes focused intently on the cage, Felicia motions for her sister to be quiet. Jan comes running back with the blanket.

In the open cage, Tom, still yelling out in pain, begins to rapidly grow. Seeing this, the aggressive cat hisses and takes off. Leaping out of the cage, it scampers down the hall.

All eyes are on Tom as he continues to transform into a human. Jeannie's mouth drops open.

JEANNIE

... I... I don't believe it.

Tom begins to groan out in pain as he reaches his full size and finds himself squished within the small cage. One of his arms and a foot are hanging out. Turning his head, he pokes it out of the cage.

TOM

Felicia! You did it. You remembered.

Taking the blanket from Jan, Felicia steps forward as Tom pulls himself out of the cage. Jeannie quickly covers Jan's eyes.

JEANNIE

Don't look honey.

Taking the blanket, Tom quickly wraps it around himself.

FELICIA

(to Tom)

I did. I don't know how but I did.

Dumbstruck, Jeannie cannot believe what she has seen. Jan and Christopher begin to tug on her arms.

JAN

See, we told you Aunt Jeannie, we told you.

CHRISTOPHER

Mom was a cat. Mom was a cat.

A confused smile slowly curls up Jeannie's face.

JEANNIE
Yeah, I... I guess she was.

TOM
Well, now that this whole thing is over... Would you still like to... You know...

FELICIA
(eager)
What?

The sun's early morning rays of light shine in through the windows behind them, brightening their faces. Blinking their eyes, they suddenly look confused.

TOM
Wha... What am I doing here? Do I know you?

FELICIA
I... I don't know. I - I feel like I do.

TOM
Me too, it's the strangest thing.

Obviously attracted to Felicia, he smiles and extends a hand to her.

TOM

My name's Tom.

Felicia smiles and they shake.

FELICIA

I'm Felicia.

Noticing that he is wearing a blanket, Tom becomes even more confused.

TOM

Wha... What happened to my clothes?

In a state of bewilderment, Felicia chuckles.

FELICIA

I don't know but I'll help you find some. Come on.

They start down the corridor leaving Jeannie and the children behind. Jan and Christopher smile.

CHRISTOPHER
Is he going to be our new dad?

JAN
I think so.

Jeannie smiles.

JEANNIE
Well, it looks like your mom's finally found her Prince Charming. And she didn't have to kiss a frog to do it... Only save a cat.

EXT. VETERINARIAN OFFICE - DAWN

The rising sun is beautiful. The symbol of something new.

ENDING CREDITS BEGIN.

They continue until **ENDING CREDITS END.**

FADE OUT

A Note from the Author

The screenplay *Meow* was written over a long July fourth weekend in 1992, in Venice, California, at the kitchen table of 1629 Penmar Ave, Apt. 3, a second floor two bedroom Lincoln Place apartment shared at that time by the script's two authors, who had recently driven across the country from Connecticut to California to pursue careers in Hollywood.

An early style word processor was pushed back and forth across the table, each author taking his turn typing as they talked out the story aloud, the scenes unfolding easily under their imaginative, creative collaboration. It was fun.

The screenplay was later pitched over the phone to production companies and studios this way:

"This is a story about a woman who is raising her two children alone. Although recognizing her children's need for a father and her need for romance, she is unable to find the right man. All of this changes one night when she transforms into a cat. As a cat, the audience can hear her thoughts as it bears witness to her struggle to find a way to turn back into a human. Along the way, she meets her Prince Charming and manages to get her children and her sister involved in her unusual adventure. It's a charming, fun-filled fantasy for the entire family. (This script is written for the cats in the film to be rendered utilizing CGI effects—computer-generated-imagery.)"

The script has not been sold; a *Meow* film has not yet been made.

The co-author Niko, who is publishing *Meow* as a surprise to its co-author Taylor, would like to take this opportunity to say:

"For over three decades, while pursuing our individual and joint creative endeavors, Taylor and I positively and stoically endured hardships, frustrations, and disappointments. It was Taylor's genuine appreciation for my writing and artwork and creative collaboration that made the early, very difficult years easier to bear. I'm thankful to him for this, and also for his unbounded enthusiasm and his never-give-up attitude. It was a fun and memorable experience collaborating with Taylor on *Meow,* our first script written together, and on the creative endeavors that followed: the screenplay *Signing With Sam*—the title later shortened to simply *Sign*—and the Upside Down Animals children's picture book series—which Taylor created and authored and to which I contributed the initial first edition artwork and character appearances for the first 16 titles of the series. "—Niko Zinovii

Niko Zinovii
Santa Monica, California
30 March 2023

niko@zinoviiartstudio.com

www.zinoviiartstudio.com

www.ingramcontent.com/pod-product-compliance
Lightning Source LLC
Chambersburg PA
CBHW031323170626
46807CB00002B/540

* 9 7 8 0 9 9 0 0 0 8 5 5 2 *